SCOTTISH
SHORT STORIES

As Stewart Conn says in his introduction, this volume is persuasive evidence that the Scottish short story, that much maligned beastie, is alive and kicking. The seventeen writers represented here draw their inspiration from as wide a spectrum as ever and present, through sharp contrasts of mood and method, a whole range of human experience. Here is life in the dead-end streets of Glasgow, and dreams distilled of Paris; childhood hopes and adult regrets; a dead mouse and a very live rat; a magician, an abduction, and a youth with cardboard shoes. Original, funny, evocative, sad – each story, finely focused, is a lens through which we look at life.

This collection is the thirteenth in the annual series published by the Scottish Arts Council and William Collins and, as before, includes an intriguing mix of new and familiar names. There will be the inevitable comparisons with past volumes, but more exciting are the challenges of the future: writers are setting themselves new targets, breaking new ground, and long may they continue to do so.

SCOTTISH SHORT STORIES

1985

Introduction by Stewart Conn

COLLINS
8 Grafton Street, London W1
1985

William Collins Sons & Co. Ltd
London · Glasgow · Sydney · Auckland
Toronto · Johannesburg

First published 1985

'Paris' by Ronald Frame also appears in *Watching Mrs Gordon* by Ronald
Frame, published by The Bodley Head.

'A Traveller's Room' by Elspeth Davie also appears in her new collection, *A Traveller's Room*, published by Hamish Hamilton.

The Publisher acknowledges the financial assistance of the Scottish Arts
Council in the publication of this volume.

BRITISH LIBRARY CATALOGUING IN PUBLICATION DATA
Scottish short stories. – 1985
1. Short stories, English – Scottish authors
2. English fiction – 20th century
823'.01'089411[FS]   PR8675
ISBN 0-00-222935-X
ISBN 0-00-222965-X Pbk

Photoset in Linotron Baskerville by
Rowland Phototypesetting Ltd
Bury St Edmunds, Suffolk
Made and printed in Great Britain by
William Collins Sons & Co. Ltd, Glasgow

CONTENTS

INTRODUCTION

Before editing this volume, I had qualms. What would be the quality of the entries, and how great the task of reading them? What might be the implications, and impositions, of there being not a sole arbiter but a panel of three? As it turned out my fears were unfounded.

For a start nothing could blunt the pleasure of responding spontaneously to work that was well written and capable of creating a world of its own, into which I was drawn. Nor was there, in subsequent discussion, any suggestion of personal preferences being put up for barter or treated as hostages to fortune. No individual favourite, that is to say, was excluded.

I was at the same time reassured by the degree of consensus where Anne Smith, Ariane Goodman and myself were concerned. This is not to imply collusion. Quite simply, we appeared to share an unspoken regard for the virtues of economy and clarity, originality and daring in the use of language, and the power to stimulate – and capture – the imagination.

Without this element of unanimity, my faith in the value of objective criteria would I think have been undermined; and those writers whose stories were to be included, and indeed the anthology itself, demeaned.

There will no doubt be comparisons between this selection and its predecessors. Rather than equate one year's crop with another, I would prefer to acknowledge the value of a series in which writers, known and about to be known, rub shoulders as equals and are enabled to reach the public they require.

This contributes towards a climate in which the very finest

talent – through its precision and perception, able to stun and illumine – is most likely to emerge and gain recognition.

What is important is that eligible writers should, from year to year, not merely continue to submit, but set themselves fresh targets; without a constant breaking of new ground and sense of challenge, there remains a danger of sameness, of narrowing perimeters.

SCOTTISH SHORT STORIES 1985, not obligatorily Scottish but firmly and fittingly so in spirit and emphasis, is persuasive evidence that the Scottish short story, that much maligned beastie, is alive and kicking. This volume has, I believe, vitality and variety. There is a healthy mix between new and familiar names. Nor was this contrived: the unknowns had to win their spurs, while Elspeth Davie, Iain Crichton Smith and Douglas Dunn are here on merit, not reputation.

A strand of continuity and quality is provided by writers included both last year and this – but with contributions which delightfully vary.

Some stories, chosen in their own right, are the pick of this or that mode. 'Friday's Child' affected me almost physically, whereas others with a similar setting and concern, but without its control, left me cold. 'Paris' conjures up a particular milieu (maybe not the one you expect!) with a finesse and delicacy missing in many submissions, for all their meticulous detail.

There are sharp contrasts of mood and method. 'The Abduction of Elvan Ratho', intricately structured and alluringly lit, lingers in the memory. 'Magician', its imagery bright and zany, makes a direct impact. At the end of 'When the Hard Rain Falls' I held my breath, lest I should disturb its stillness.

There are adult fears and childhood imaginings. There are attempts, with differing degrees of success, to get off with girls. There are shoes with cardboard soles, a dead mouse, and an extremely live rat. A first-person confession resonates disconcertingly. A baby burbles, surrealistically, 'like an unintelligible phone'. One woman is luxuriously 'liquid with hope, deliquescent with longing'; while another wanders Edinburgh 'in an opera cloak, floppy blue hat and cow-bells, like part of a school crocodile separated somehow from the main body'.

It would not be fair to say which story had me laughing out loud: this would preclude the joy of personal discovery. In any case, I mention those I do not to exclude the others, but to whet the appetite.

Real thanks are due to everyone who submitted stories; and to the Scottish Arts Council and William Collins, the thirteenth in whose annual series this astonishingly is. May you, the reader, find much enjoyment in it.

STEWART CONN

THE ABDUCTION OF ELVAN RATHO

Scoular Anderson

'There are only five lines,' Duncan Ratho announced.

'What does it matter?' said his wife, counting the stitches on her knitting needle.

'Less than last year,' said Ratho.

'It's the same as last year. It's exactly the same diary as last year.'

'Five lines isn't much space for the thoughts of the day.'

His wife silently rearranged her wool.

'It's not much space, really, in which to record the events of the day from seven-thirty in the morning to eleven at night.'

'It's enough for you. More than enough.'

'In fact, it's longer than that. I could possibly formulate some great thought at six while still lying in bed waiting for the alarm to go off – or, for that matter, at one o'clock in the morning when I can't get to sleep. Thoughts that come into your head at that time might be the most interesting thoughts of your life – though I suppose that thoughts at one o'clock in the morning belong to the next day, if you see what I mean.' He laughed lightly at his own joke while his wife's knitting needles clicked on humourlessly.

After some minutes of silence in which Duncan Ratho travelled hither and thither through the diary as if checking that all the days were there, pen poised uncapped in his hand, and his wife's knitting had expanded fluffily another inch, she said:

'It's exactly the same diary as last year. Elvan always gives you the same diary on your birthday.'

'I suppose it is,' he said, returning to the day in which he sat,

January the ninth, his birthday. On one side of him the giant gas fire pumped out its luxuriant heat while on the other, the occasional whiff of whisky came pleasurably drifting from the tumbler on the table.

'She hasn't rung you. Elvan always rings you on your birthday,' said his wife.

'I expect she's busy. She'll be out on the town somewhere. You know what it's like at university.' Having inherited his father's business, Ratho had not been to university. The life of hard learning and vivacious living was his rather idealized image of it. 'You can't expect her to arrange her life round a five-minute phone call.'

'Five minutes isn't asking much.'

'No. But she will have other things to do.' He felt a twinge of disappointment and imagined that these were the pinpricks that all parents must dread – the little family traditions dying out. However, one tradition which looked as if it would never die out, though he wished it would, was the diary birthday present. Wrapped in tasteful paper, it always appeared on his birthday breakfast table. It was like some sort of punishment his daughter had decided he must receive, not just on his birthday, but on every day of the year. The white yawn of the diary mocked the emptiness of his days because Duncan Ratho could never think what to write in it.

'All my life should be here!' he said aloud, suddenly.

His wife looked up, briefly surprised.

'I should be able to look back through all my diaries and remind myself of the more interesting or important happenings in our life.'

'Such as?'

'Do you remember the fifty-three rooks on that roundabout on the way back from wherever it was? I was astounded by so many black birds sitting quite the thing, with the traffic roaring round them. I drove round the roundabout three times so that I could count them. Elvan was so embarrassed.' He remembered his daughter tap-tapping on his shoulder, her sharp finger tapping, her face red with humiliation.

'What's so important about that? That's just a silly reminisc-
ence,' said his wife.

'She was so innocent then, Elvan. Just a girl. So gawky and
unsure of herself.' In a drawer somewhere he had dozens of
cinefilms of Elvan as a baby, a child, a schoolgirl. One day, he
kept promising himself, he would edit them on to one long reel.

Ratho shrugged. He knew his diary would never contain
personal theories on world affairs, frank opinions on those
around him or even secret, passionate jottings. All there would
ever be was the temperature, which is what he always ended up
noting in his diary, written in his fountain-penned scrawl, an
esoteric symbol beneath the date.

His wife put down her knitting and switched on the radio.

'What are you going to listen to?' he asked, his heart already
sinking, already sensing the answer.

'An opera.'

He sighed, sitting back into the soft, whispering chair.

'Puccini,' said his wife with almost a smack of lips.

Ratho wondered whether he should take the dog out for a
walk or go and lie in a hot bath – anything rather than suffer the
torture of another opera. He had spent a large amount of his life
sitting in his chair pretending to read a newspaper or a book
and listening to the incomprehensible plodding chords stamp
about the room. The notes lashed and ripped at his skin,
passionate coloratura actually got under it, irritating his bones.
It might have been better if he could understand the absurd
plots. He took a large gulp of whisky and settled himself down
with the contents of his diary again, starting at the beginning:
*Personal information. Lighting-up times. Handy conversion table of
weights and measures.*

Ascension Day. Shrove Tue. Ash Wed.

The names whirled in Arthur Quilt's head, a strange prayer.
Quinquagesima. First after Epiphany.

'You are a filter,' Old George said to him, and that whirled
about in his head, too, until he had pinned it down by setting in
his diary among the other strange words.

You are a filter, Old George said Arthur Quilt wrote in his diary and remembered discs of filter paper in science classes at school, white cones filled with crystals, crucibles boiling in their vapour producing gritty salt. On her top lip, his science teacher wore a painted cupid's bow, bravely arched, the scarlet bare in places where the wild lips clutched at cigarettes. Filter tips. Filter feeders. The basking shark is a filter feeder, the science teacher once told him. It swims lazily around with its jaws open wide filtering minute food particles from the water. It seemed to Arthur that something similar had happened to him at school but he had spent his time filtering out useless bits of information while the real, meaty chunks of knowledge had gone floating by.

Old George had eyed him up and down suspiciously when he reported for the job.

'This week, I'll show you what's what, then you'll be on your own.' Old George glanced at the gold stud in Arthur Quilt's left ear. 'You are a filter. You are here to intercept calls and callers. You are here to protect the stars of the opera from any old riff-raff that comes a'calling. Whether the person telephones or comes here to the stage door, you must be able to *discern*. Do you get my meaning?' George looked again at the gold stud. 'You let some people through, you keep out the rest. Those you let through you direct to the appropriate dressing-room. Tact is what you need, lad. Have you got plenty of tact?' George waited for some reaction, got none, so spread another heading, banner-like between them. 'Bouquets and telegrams. On the first night you are responsible for delivering bouquets and telegrams to the dressing-rooms. Always knock and wait to be called.'

Arthur Quilt's pale face remained unmoved.

'My God,' said George, 'it's like driving nails into a piece of timber. Now plants. *My* plants.' He rotated several degrees so that his large stomach pointed in the direction of three flower pots on the windowsill. 'Water them once a week. *Water*, not drown.'

Arthur looked at the plants, smug bunches of green and mauve. They would be the ones to tell tales, he decided. Old

George showed him how to work the switchboard then felt free to relax for a moment or two.

'I'm off to visit my niece in Florida. She's paying my fare. I shall be able to walk about in my shirt-sleeves next week, oh yes. They have alligators in Florida, you know.' George rattled his dentures in anticipation. 'But at the moment I am going out to buy a paper and you are in charge. A bit of practice won't do any harm.'

So Arthur Quilt, five feet eight inches tall, red-haired, his pectorals totally undeveloped, gaps between his teeth, a school certificate in biology and another in woodwork, became, for a time at least, the Keeper of the Door. He was aware of the awesome responsibility from the start. *You are a filter.* The kidney is a filter, the lung an exchange surface, his science teacher said. Or was it the other way around? So much knowledge accumulated in little broken scraps. People came and went through the door with great purpose, ignoring what Arthur Quilt thought was a challenging look in his eye. He boiled Old George's kettle and made a cup of coffee. He poured the remainder of the boiled water in the kettle into the plant pots. He filled up the day's space in his diary. He wrote that Old George was a pompous git and made an observation on opera-singers' lungs which, when in full flight, he imagined to be like the distended, almost transparent throats of bellowing frogs and when at rest, like shrivelled party balloons. He read the newspaper from cover to cover, staring especially hard at his horoscope, desiring that the vague words would at last mean something hopeful.

From above, down the dark stairwell, came notions of another world – a heaven or a hell – somewhere ablaze with lights or damped in darkness: scraps of music, scales, hammer-blows, shouts, the whirring of stage machinery. Unknown to Arthur the signs of the zodiac, picked out in gold, bordered a giant disc suspended in a black void. On the disc gods and goddesses stepped elegantly through their feuds, lovers changed partners, changed partners again and gently perspired under elaborate clothes.

15

Arthur Quilt scratched at the crotch of his trousers, put the kettle on again and fingered the plastic cover of his new diary, the first diary he had ever owned, a school-leaving present from an aunt. He read through what he had already written and could hardly wait for a new day into which he could write more.

As Duncan Ratho pulled back the curtain to look at the thermometer suspended in the darkness outside the window, the two diarists met. Arthur Quilt saw Ratho's head, a dark silhouette against the lavish light of the sitting room while Ratho saw Quilt's face, a pale moon with its attendant satellite earring, orbitting past in the dark garden.

'There's a boy,' said Ratho, turning round. His wife's knitting lay on her lap, her eyes were closed but the rapturous smile on her lips gave sterner warning against interruption.

'There's a boy in the garden,' said Ratho more loudly. His wife's expression turned from sweet to sour, her eyes clicked open.

'You seem to have a marvellous knack at interrupting an opera at the most crucial moments.' She sighed loudly and looked almost apologetically at the radio. The singers continued unaware. The sitting room door was flung open and in ran Elvan, arms wide to scoop up as much of her father's baggy cardigan as possible, to cuddle the comforting plumpness of his middle age. The opera was completely drowned out by the dog bounding and whining with glee, her tail cracking at the furniture.

'Happy birthday, Daddy-o!'

'Elvan! What are you doing here?' Ratho tried to mask his delight.

'I've come to wish you a happy birthday.'

In the doorway behind Elvan's head Ratho noticed the two boys, the one with the pale face who had just passed the window, and another one with several earrings and a wild, windswept-looking hairstyle.

'Who are they?' he asked.

'The other part of the singing telegram. Right, boys, from the top . . . Happy birthday to you . . .' Elvan's sweet voice sang alone. The boys stared. Mrs Ratho, casting aside opera and knitting, stood up to peck her daughter on the cheek. Ratho considered that his wife had encouraged their daughter to have good looks, a recalcitrant nature and a politely insolent manner. He imagined it had been forced on a rather plain and gentle child. He sometimes worried about how he himself had influenced her.

'Have you eaten?' Mrs Ratho asked Elvan.

'Now don't start fussing, Mum.'

Parents were never right, could never be right, Duncan Ratho reflected. They brought up their children in what they considered the right way but they would later see in their offspring's adult smile or tilt of head or certain confidence of limbs all sorts of glaring discrepancies or grudges. The two boys had parents, too, no doubt. Had they done any better? he wondered.

'Who are your friends, Elvan?' his wife asked.

'This is Chiz and Quiltie. Chiz is forming his own band. Quiltie's got a job. Actually,' Elvan plucked a grape or two from the bunch lying in the bowl on the coffee table and popped them in her mouth, 'what I really came home for was to pick up one or two of my things. My digs are a bit bare.'

Ratho saw Elvan's white teeth puncture the grapes and his feelings were mauled along with them.

'See you anon,' said Elvan going out, followed by her attendants.

Sitting down again, Mrs Ratho turned up the volume of the radio and frowned into her knitting. Ratho rechecked the thermometer and noted the temperature in his diary. He could have written much more, he knew, tonight of all nights. He could have recorded the fact that his daughter had arrived on his birthday with strange friends. He could have written how he did not like the look of them, how Elvan was so innocent. He could have dug right down to the feelings he sensed were swarming somewhere inside him but he knew he could never refine them into words.

17

'*My name is Tubifex, I am vice-filter of the twelfth volume, that is to say, the volume which contains the lower galaxies. Having indoctrinated the earth-girl Elvan, she promised to take us to her house of origin. She comes from a family unit of three, her male parent being wealthy owner of a surgical dressings factory.*' Quilt flicked through his diary. Elvan had taken them upstairs to her bedroom where the colours smacked of childhood. Posters of pop stars, now scorned, were still attached to the walls. Little crumbs of an earlier life lay on the shelves and window ledges – teddy bears, the torso of a doll, a colouring book. Together they laughed at some old photographs, smoked a cigarette. Chiz removed Elvan's clothes and Elvan removed Chiz's and together they slipped under the bright flowers of Elvan's duvet. Quilt lounged in an armchair reading his diary. From time to time he saw Chiz's buttocks languidly surfacing like the brows of porpoises.

'*I, Tubifex,*' he wrote in his diary, '*and comrade vice-filter Chiz have decided to put Plan Z into action: the Abduction of Elvan Ratho.*' Or was it adduction? The adductors draw together, the abductors draw apart, his science teacher said, disconnecting with a click the skin from a plastic model. The muscles were exposed, painted in violent purples and reds, folded in upon one another like the tight growth of a vegetable. Later, the teacher made him stand in front of the class while she pointed out the muscles on his body. He felt the embarrassing pressure of her hand on his thigh, smelled her smoky breath and had a pang of irrational panic as he imagined her detaching his leg with ease. He wrote in his diary a description of his science teacher. He wrote about how he had gone into her classroom one lunchtime to retrieve his bag and found her sitting at her desk, a cigarette in her hand, gazing into a mug of coffee and crying. She was dabbing her nose with a ball of tissue. Just when you thought you had somebody taped, he noted, they would suddenly do something *amazing*, like crying into their coffee. After you had spent years loathing some old bat who said you smelled and then squirted aerosol freshener in the air-space above your head, she would suddenly burst out crying and get you embarrassed. He wondered if Elvan's parents would cry when they abducted their daughter and demanded the money. He went over the plan again, noting it down in his diary, fearful lest Chiz should think him incompetent.

Chiz arose from under the duvet, apparently refreshed.

'How about a cup of coffee?'

Elvan propped herself up on the pillow.

'Quiltie, friend. Nip down to the kitchen and put on the kettle. Coffee's in the cupboard above the sink. Milk in the fridge. Sugar in the blue bowl on dresser. Mugs on hooks third cupboard from window. Perhaps biccies in box by the cooker.'

Quilt moved off down the stairs and firstly, by mistake, into the sitting room where he was hit by Puccini. He saw the parents, wearing disconcerted expressions, bent over knitting and diary. He reversed out, tried the next door – a darkened dining room containing the warm, slightly scented aura of a recently consumed meal. At last, to the gentle pinging of fluorescent tubes, the kitchen awakened in a blaze of lights. He began opening cupboards. *Ground Almonds, Whole Almonds, Peppercorns Black, Peppercorns Green.* Mrs Ratho's formidable collection of comestibles darted at his eyes. He had never seen the like. *Coffee Beans. Coffee Filters.* More knowledge of doubtful value, he supposed, etched forever on his brain. The appendix, he learned in science, was a mysterious organ of the body which sometimes filled up with detritus, grape-pips for example, and had to be removed. He wondered if something similar could happen to the brain – some portion of it having to be sliced off, inflamed by an excess of useless knowledge.

'Can I help you?' Duncan Ratho stood in the doorway, glasses in one hand, diary in the other.

'I was told to make coffee.'

Duncan Ratho came into the kitchen, laying down diary and glasses, thinking that the boy looked harmless enough but somehow made him feel uncomfortable.

'Ground or instant?'

'Eh?'

'Here, I'll do it.' He filled the kettle. 'Where did you say you worked?'

'At the Opera.'

Ratho could forgive him that.

'Your parents must be pleased that you've got a job.'

'Dunno. Suppose so.'

'Parents worry about these things, you know.'

'Don't know what they think.' Quilt seemed to shrug at the memory of a mother and father.

'We worry about Elvan. She seems so young, if you know what I mean.' Quilt was trying to picture his parents worrying about him.

'We had hoped that Elvan would find good friends at university, mix with fellow students. It can be very stimulating, you know. Exchange of ideas and all that. I never went to university. I don't think I was really the type.' Ratho poured water swirlingly into three mugs.

'I've got a diary like yours,' said Arthur Quilt suddenly. He had been staring at Ratho's diary for some time, amazed that a middle-aged, well-off stranger should own an identical plastic-covered diary to his own.

'A birthday present from Elvan.'

Arthur Quilt had pulled his own diary from his back pocket and was fanning the pages proudly. 'Look. Exactly the same.' He felt fellowship oozing in his ribs like the sudden friendship generated by the chance meeting of owners of a rare breed of dog. Ratho looked enviously and uncomfortably at the pages, black with the dancing scrawl of words.

'I never had much time for diary-writing,' he said sharply.

Arthur Quilt then leaned closely towards him. 'I think I must warn you,' he said in a dramatic whisper.

'Pardon?'

'We plan . . . Chiz plans to abduct your daughter.' Quilt felt suddenly better. Ratho looked at the pale, thin face apparently lacking any sense of humour.

'If I know Elvan, she'll scream the house down.' He laughed and held out the tray.

Quilt walked upstairs feeling feeble, hurt by his own naivety. It seemed the train of events was not that easy to stop. Elvan and Chiz were submerged under the duvet again so he laid down the tray and went out to find the bog.

In the Rathos' bedroom he felt he could hardly breathe, so dense were the furnishings. The carpets, the curtains, the wall-to-wall cupboards jostled with each other in a bid to exclude intruders. Arthur entered brazenly, padded round the bed, lifted the lid of Ratho's executive case with his toe, saw pens tucked in a row, inside-out newspapers, a copy of *Playboy*. 'Dirty old letch,' he whispered. Music swelled passionately somewhere below him, the digital clock by the bed clicked on another minute. He opened a wardrobe door and saw his own image dart darkly past in a long mirror. He fingered Ratho's selection of striped silk ties. In the bathroom he stripped off, plucked thoughtfully at various parts of his flesh then stood under the shower until the hot water grew tepid. 'Snoop around,' Chiz had said. 'Find out their weakness. We could use it for blackmail.' Now Arthur Quilt was becoming tired of this game. Elvan's father seemed all right, not the kind that he would want to cause harm to. With a towel round his waist he sat on the edge of the bath and transferred his thoughts to his diary. He had now overflowed out of the correct day's space, and the next day's, and would soon be in the next week's. It no longer seemed to matter.

'Where have you been?' demanded Chiz when Quilt returned to Elvan's room reeking of a cocktail of lotions and sprays, his hair hanging in damp rats' tails. Chiz was sitting cross-legged on the bed while Elvan was surrounding one of his eyes with a design of swooping cusps using her own make-up.

'Chiz wants to be different,' Elvan said. Chiz pushed her aside.

'Come on, Quiltie, remember we have things to arrange.' The made-up eye winked, quivered like an exotic insect. In the centre of the colour, Quiltie saw something cold.

'Chiz, I think this is a mistake,' he said.

'Shut your mouth.'

21

Elvan stuffed one or two bits and pieces in her bag and they paraded downstairs. Duncan Ratho came to the sitting room door wearing what he hoped was a benign smile. Elvan paused to kiss her father.

'Sorry I can't stay, Chiz's old banger turns into a pumpkin at midnight. I'll try and get home in a fortnight for a proper visit.' She peered over his shoulder at the back of her mother's head. 'I see Mum has her head in the arias. Give her a kiss from me.'

Ratho closed the door behind them, feeling as though he was guillotining a piece of film. The piece with Elvan on it was slithering quickly away, never to be included in that big reel he always planned to make. He was rather disappointed in her choice of friends, of course. The one called Chiz he distrusted and disliked but it was a straightforward feeling. The one called Quiltie made him uneasy. As the boy passed by in the hall he smelled strongly and sweetly of something unidentifiably familiar. He had the look in his eye of someone who knew too much.

Ratho returned to his chair in the sitting room. The opera had finished. His wife looked at him brightly, the music having enlivened her.

'I never understand how a story of anguish, betrayal and probably death can actually refresh someone's spirits,' he said.

'Don't be silly, Duncan. It's the music that counts. Where's Elvan?'

'She's gone.'

'Gone?'

'A minute or two ago.'

'But why didn't you tell me? Oh, Duncan, why did you let her go without letting me know?'

'Because you were engrossed in your silly, bloody opera.'

The knitting-needles began to move again, stabbing furiously at the wool.

Arthur Quilt, Keeper of the Door, filled a milk bottle with water and sloshed some into each plant pot. Old George's pets seemed without joy, held no surprises, were content to get on with the job of living. He had never been able to grasp the theory of photosynthesis. All he could remember clearly was the word, or rather, his science teacher's method of pronouncing it, her red lips pursing, stretching, kissing as she parcelled out each syllable for easy consumption. Leaves took in something, changed something, gave out something else. Filters. Filtering light or gasses, changing fart and bad breath into sweet, fresh air. Their leaves sucked in at one end, their roots did the same at the other, day and night, non-stop. He looked closely again at the plants, marvelling how such sullen clumps camouflaged their constant activity.

He sat down and opened his diary, smoothing flat the pages ready to write.

Elvan had not screamed the house down. In fact, when Chiz announced to her that she was going to be tied up, locked in a room and not released until her father paid the ransom demanded of him, she laughed and seemed eager to co-operate with any outlandish plans Chiz had for her. Chiz became disconcerted and swore a lot, worked himself up until he almost screamed, changed his plan several times.

Eventually, to hide his tears, he lifted up his guitar, bent his body over it and began picking at the strings. Unamplified, they whispered tinnily.

'I mean, you can't abduct a friend,' said Elvan.

Chiz picked.

'What do you want to do this for anyway?' Elvan sat down opposite him, resting her elbows on her knees. Quilt saw her skirt ride up, exposing her long thighs. Chiz continued to pick.

'What are you going to do with the money?' asked Elvan.

'I don't want his fucking money!' said Chiz throwing the guitar aside. 'I want . . .' Impossible to describe, Chiz knew what he wanted. It was simple. He wanted to create and destroy, he wanted to make his mark. He wanted to wire his bass guitar into the nearest pylon, to pluck the strings as if they were an archer's bow, to feel the tension and its release as the notes sped away like arrows. He wanted to sound notes so low, to reach down and down below music and timbre so that people would hear nothing yet feel a sharp throbbing in their spines. He wanted notes with the strength of missiles so that buildings would crack. His music would spark from pylon to pylon across the entire national grid. From one end of the country to the other his riff would enter people's homes so that their radios, kettles, hairdriers, lawnmowers would vibrate with music until they were red hot. There would be no escape. Even lovers would be accompanied by the song of their electric blankets. Having made his mark, Chiz would be happy.

Arthur Quilt had already made his mark. This thing of his, this diary, the gold lettering on the cover already worn away, the corners curling, the pages filled up almost to the middle of the last month although he was still living in the middle of the first, this was his mark. No one need see it. Knowing the powers of his private creation was satisfying enough. Reading through it was like diving under water into a world that moved at a slower pace, familiar yet silent, decked out in strange colours. Between the pages of the diary he had described and wondered, thrown insults, reminisced with enemies, made love to Elvan, coaxing from his virgin flesh and experienced imagination better pleasures than Chiz offered, he was sure. Closing the diary was like surfacing into bedlam.

'You're in trouble, boy, I'm telling you that now!'

Duncan Ratho had thrust his head and shoulders through the enquiries hatch in front of Quilt.

'I want an explanation of this.' Ratho reached into his jacket pocket and pulled out a piece of paper, pinning it to the table in front of Quilt with a stabbing finger. Quilt looked down at the letter in his own handwriting, dictated by Elvan and Chiz. How could he explain that the pair of them were probably sitting drinking coffee in Elvan's digs at that very moment and this piece of paper was meant to be what they called a symbolic gesture.

'It's a joke,' he eventually said weakly.

'A demand for twenty thousand pounds, a joke?' Ratho looked as if he was going to force himself right through the hatch.

'Where is Elvan? I want her handed over to me *now*.'

'I don't know where she is.'

'If she is not here beside me, unharmed, within five minutes, I'm going to call the police.'

'I don't know where she is,' Quilt repeated without conviction, hoping that she had not in fact gone home with Chiz and could presently be summoned from the shadows of the hall.

'We'll see about this,' said Ratho, withdrawing from the hatch and heading for the stairs. Quilt leapt from his chair. 'You can't go up there. There's a rehearsal on.' He opened the door of the room and ran after Ratho. *You are a filter*, Old George had said.

Ratho followed steps, corridors, pushed his way through doors, sure that he would be able to catch the scent of his daughter, smell her innocence, her gullibility, her fear seeping out under some door and offer her protection. In the darkness he caught glimpses of surprised faces or restraining hands. He flew at columns of cloth and gauze. Why was everything steeped in infuriating darkness? As his anger began to subside he remembered Hamlet's uncle, calling for lights when confronted with the truth.

It was only when the music stopped that he realized there had been music at all. Instruments drew untidily to a halt.

'Who's that moving about the stage?' a distant voice called.

The lights came on so brightly that Ratho was plunged from one sort of blindness into another.

'Who the hell's *that*?' the voice bellowed again. 'Get him off the stage!'

Now bewildered, Ratho shouted back.

'I demand to see my daughter!'

'Will someone escort that gentleman off the stage, please. We'll have to start again.'

Members of the orchestra began to stand up for a better view. Near Ratho, figures in elaborate costumes looked around in puzzlement. The perspiring face of Duncan Ratho bathed in dazzling light shot a questioning glance at the dark silhouette of Quilt – the ears were recognizable – standing in the wings. He could not see the boy's eyes but he imagined them feasting on his stupidity with their curious, acquisitive gaze.

Much later Ratho sent his same questioning glance at Elvan when she appeared in the sitting room. Parents must be the most bewildered humans on earth, he decided, doomed always to be caught out. But Elvan seemed as much surprised by the loss of her innocence as he was. After the arguments, the shouting and the tears, Ratho searched for some tiny link that would bridge the gulf suddenly grown between them.

'Promise me one thing, Elvan. You will continue to send me a diary on my birthday, won't you?'

'I promise, Daddy-o.'

DIRTY TEX

William Andrew

Impatiently he allowed his mother to button him into his navy blue raincoat. He had already pointed out the brightness of the June evening. The sun still shone on the front windows of their top-storey flat, a shaft of light from his bedroom piercing the gloom of the little hall where they stood, and beyond the windows the narrow streets of grey tenements still held the day's heat like the firebricks in the kitchen grate when he cleaned out the previous night's cinders.

He knew better than to go on arguing when her face had that set, half-resentful look to it, and her hands moved so roughly that he staggered as she tugged each button to its buttonhole. Her eyes and her hands said here she was, a lonely widow who had been working all day in a stuffy city store, dealing with hot, bad-mannered customers, and now that she was home there was the house to clean; *she* couldn't go out to play just because the sun shone. Being fitted into his raincoat, her insistence implied, was a small price to pay for missing his share of the evening's chores.

'Who are you going to play with?' She asked the inevitable question, stooping over him for the lowest button, so that he could smell the cologne she always dabbed on her temples and throat when she came home from the shop.

'Peter and Stuart,' he said promptly, naming the second-top and third-top boys in his class.

'And where are you going to play?'

'In the park.'

They were, in fact, to meet in an area of scrubland known locally as the Bluebell Wood, which was further from home than she liked him to stray in the evening. The park was only two blocks away. Since it was a lie, he directed it not at her face but at the hallstand and wondered if she had noticed. She usually did.

'And when are you going to be back?'

'Eight o'clock.'

'Eight o'clock sharp, or you don't go out tomorrow evening. And if you have to ask somebody the time, ask the park keeper or a policeman or a lady.'

With this familiar warning, which carried hints of dangers he did not understand, she released him. He had the front door open on the cat-and-disinfectant smell of the stair when she called, 'Nigel!' He turned, She was caught in the beam of light from his room, a stout, already greying figure in a purple overall, her face featureless in the glare, though her voice indicated her stern expression. 'The park, remember. You promised.'

He nodded, closed the door and raced downstairs to erase the memory of his promise. When he reached the street, she was at the sitting room window. He looked up and waved, and she waved back, and he knew she would stay there until he was out of sight. He walked sedately to the corner, looked back to give a last reassuring wave and turned left as if he were going to the park. But as soon as he knew she could not see, he turned right into another canyon of stone and glass and doubled back towards the forbidden land, breaking into a run as he did so. With an exhilarating sense of freedom and betrayal he tore off his raincoat and fastened it round his neck by the top button to form a cape which he hoped would be appropriate to whatever game they would be playing.

The Bluebell Wood was a hillside which had proved too steep to build on, a wide slope of grass and bushes and a few trees, scattered with dark boulders and criss-crossed by paths which took exciting dips and turns; it could be a prairie or a jungle or a planet unexplored by man. Now for the boy it shone bright and newly green, and full of the expectation of company and adventure as he wandered from one warm clearing to another. Gradually, however, the expectation began to fade. He met only one or two adults walking their dogs. It would not be the first time that Peter and Stuart had changed their plans at short notice and not bothered to tell him. Perhaps he should have borrowed Jock, the downstairs neighbour's black and white mongrel, always a more reliable companion than any human.

He was sitting on a rock, plaiting grass and planning not to speak to his two friends next day in school, when he heard a group of boys approaching. Joyfully he ran to meet them and found that Peter and Stuart were among them, but they barely acknowledged his greeting because also present, and therefore leader for the night, was Tommy Fox. Probably it was on his whim and not because they had to meet Nigel that they were in the wood at all. Tommy Fox was the biggest boy in their class, an alarming enigma who had two personalities: one the cowed, baffled, occasionally trouser-wetting occupant of the front desk; the other the undoubted king of the playground where, with his fawning entourage of younger boys, he delighted in organizing games of strength and endurance that showed the brightest of his classmates at their worst.

'Aw, look!' he now shouted. 'It's Niggle!' There was the customary laughter at this to which Nigel responded with the usual brave smile. He had often wondered what kind of world his parents had imagined him growing up in where such a name would be acceptable. Certainly not one shared by Tommy Fox. The leader, bulky in soiled shirt and long shorts, gathered the boys around him and explained the game they would be playing. He had seen this Western at the Embassy the other night about a new sheriff cleaning up a town. He would, of course, be the sheriff and he began to distribute the other parts. With envy Nigel heard Peter become Buck and Stuart, Lucky, and he had resigned himself to being an anonymous member of a gang when suddenly Tommy pointed a nail-bitten finger at him and declared, 'And you can be Dirty Tex.'

Dazed, Nigel murmured his thanks, and was told that he was to shoot somebody and ride off into the hills, and this would be when the new sheriff would raise his first posse and go in pursuit. Dirty Tex would be caught and shot like the rat he was.

Obviously it was not a role that would last long, but it seemed to be one that mattered.

Tommy said, 'We'll start off that we're all just going about our business and Dirty Tex walks into the store and shoots the nice old storekeeper.' The nice old storekeeper was to be the youngest boy there, someone's wee brother compulsorily attached, an infant in tartan shirt and safety-pinned pants, so new to the world that he had to be taught how to fall when shot. 'Then you ride away to your hideout, and we all come after you.'

As most of the boys started to go about their business with studied casualness, the infant was stood behind the rock which would serve as a counter. Tex swaggered towards him and, though troubled about motivation and afraid to ask, slowly raised his forefinger and fired, making convincing pistol-shot sounds as he pumped several bullets into the nice old store-keeper, who, mouth agape at the realism of it all, chose to cry instead of fall. Then Tex, slapping the flanks of his horse, his evil cloak flapping behind him, rode off out of town.

Happy in the knowledge that he still had his death scene to play, and with it a chance to show the infant how to fall clutching your wound, Nigel galloped along the familiar winding paths towards where he knew the best hideout to be. He reckoned he could prolong his participation in the game by making it really difficult for the posse to find him. The path narrowed to the barest track, and he had to edge between the tugging branches of a thicket of hawthorn.

At just the right moment he dropped to his hands and knees and crawled over damp dead leaves through a tunnel of undergrowth, heading for his secret clearing where the wood met the convent wall. Already he was planning his death, a fine, noble event in spite of Tex's foul deeds in the past, ending only after he had returned fire for several minutes. The first wound, he thought, ought to be in his shoulder, the second in his thigh and finally he would be writhing in agony as a bullet in his abdomen took its terrible toll. Even the new sheriff could not fail to be impressed by the drama of it all.

He could see the clearing now, the sun striking the grass and the faded bluebells and the boulder behind which he would take cover. Suddenly he heard voices ahead of him, two voices murmuring together. Secretly. Had the posse got there first? Out of the question. Hesitating, he put a hand down to steady himself and a thorn pierced his palm.

'Ouch!' he exclaimed, and the voices stopped.

A terrible stillness framed the next few minutes. He saw a man and a woman lying side by side on the warm grass beneath the convent wall, saw that the man's jacket was draped across their middles, saw the man raise his head to look in his direction, lower it and lie motionless, heard him say, 'Christ, two of them,' in an incredulous whisper, and the woman's giggle in reply, short and shrill, heard a rustle of leaves to his right . . . and saw, as the earth spun and his body jerked in terror, another man's face a few feet from his own, a long, white face, eyes wild with fright or anger.

For an age their stare held his, and then above him a bird chirped, and the silence shattered into panic. Nigel gave a whimper of fear and began to crawl backwards, but branches and thorns grabbed at him and caught his coat which started to gather round his neck and over his head. Beside him he could hear the breaking of twigs and the harsh snorts of breath which meant the man was also struggling to escape. Back in the clearing the man and woman laughed freely now, and there was something triumphant and mocking about their laughter which said they were now in control of the situation, somehow they had won.

Abruptly Nigel found himself in the combined nightmares of unexplained derision, desperate and impeded progress and a race against unseen danger. He sobbed as he tugged his coat free and scrambled back to the path. Where the man was waiting for him.

He had a quick shocking glimpse of a narrow, ashen face topped by a black beret, a long, thin overcoat whose sleeves did not meet the dark woollen gloves, before he felt his arm gripped and he was being rushed along the path too stunned to call out.

The man stopped, glanced back as if to make sure they were out of earshot of the couple and then bent over him to say, 'I'm not going to hurt you.' His voice was high-pitched and wheezing, his breath sour.

Nigel looked at the hand that held him. Between the glove and the cuff of the overcoat – overcoat and gloves in June? – was a thin, raw wrist from which little patches of skin flaked, white from pink. 'You were doing something bad, weren't you?' the man said, apparently pleading to be agreed with.

Forcing himself to look at the face, Nigel saw that there were areas of peeling skin there too, some flaked with dry blood, and that black, strangely wiry hair thrust wildly from under the beret. 'You were bad, weren't you?' the man insisted, and Nigel, now as scared of the man's obvious unhealthiness as he was of the fierce grip of his fingers, was beyond arguing. If this oddly dressed leper said that he had been bad, he would in the cause of an early release allow it to be true. He nodded. 'Very bad?' He nodded again, and decided he liked the man's lips least; they were full and wet and bluish.

The man stood irresolute, as if wondering if this admission were enough, and Nigel felt his fear begin to ebb. He was going to be talked to, not physically attacked, and the talking-to was taking a monotonous turn. 'You wouldn't like your mummy to know what you were doing, would you?' There was a question Nigel wanted to ask about this. What *had* he been doing that was so wicked? But he wanted to say nothing that would prolong this encounter so he shook his head. The man smiled, and Nigel thought that now he liked the teeth least of all; they were brown with grey mush near the gums. 'Then we won't tell anybody,' the man assured him. 'This will be our secret.'

'Yes, please,' Nigel said and made to go.

The hand still held him. 'Are you sure now?' The awful smile was wider now, as if some kind of friendship had been formed.

'Yes, I'm sure!' Nigel cried, tore himself away and fled. And, as he ran, reaction set in and he started to cry. Down in the darkening streets he slowed to a walk, and shook and wept. He was aware of the curiosity of passers-by but knew he could not stop and take comfort from anyone without saying what had happened. He climbed the stairs of his flat, and mopped at his eyes before letting himself in. His mother was in the sitting room and since she was using the vacuum cleaner did not hear him come in. He went into the bathroom and scrubbed at his hands and face to clear them of the terrible man's undoubted germs, and then he gargled thoroughly, sure that he must have breathed in some of the air the man had breathed out.

Later he considered going to his mother and telling her exactly what had happened, but he was afraid that she too would decide that he had done something bad and be angry with him. She might not, of course. She might draw him in against her warmth and stroke his forehead and soothe him, the way she did when he had had a fall or was running a temperature. But it was risky, and he had promised not to tell anyone. It was simpler to go into his bedroom and work on his model ship, and concentrate on forgetting, the way he had at other moments of personal crisis like the occasional bad mark at school or some humiliation at Tommy Fox's hands in the playground.

When at last he and his mother shared their supper of milk and biscuits, he was calm enough to listen carefully as she dreamily retold an episode from her childhood spent in a quiet Perthshire village where her father had kept the shop. It was the story of how, when she was very little, her purse had opened as she crossed some stepping stones, and how she had gone back day after day until she found the last halfpenny lying under a pebble in the stream. There was a moral, of course, which usually wearied him, but tonight he could only wonder at the beautiful simplicity of her childhood in which a lost halfpenny had been so important.

That night in bed the terror of the silence of these three adults in the wood returned to him, and with it questions he knew he could never ask anyone. What had he done that was so wrong? What had that couple been doing lying under that oddly placed jacket? Why had a man so obviously ill been creeping about among damp leaves under a hawthorn bush? Why had he felt so guilty when the man had accused him, when all he had been doing was hide from the posse? And later, when he had relived too often his undignified scramble through the thicket, and the soft laughter that had accompanied it, and was about to fall into a fitful sleep, the last question came to him, the answer to which he *did* know, only too well – why had the posse not appeared on the scene to help him?

The next morning in the playground, Peter admitted that as soon as Nigel had galloped off, Tommy Fox had sniggered and led the whole gang away in the opposite direction. 'What did you do?' he asked, half apologetic, half gloating. 'How long did it take you to realize we weren't coming to look for you?'

'Not long,' Nigel said. His day was being clouded and confused by the bad dreams of the night before. 'As a matter of fact, I met someone.'

'Who?'

'Dirty Tex.'

'Dirty Tex?' Peter gave him a look that said he had just confirmed his reputation as a crazy genius, and wandered off to find more congenial company.

On his way home from school that day – a day characterized by poor concentration and much surprised nagging from Miss Cunningham – Nigel stopped to look into the window of the newsagent's on the main road. There was a display of comic annuals at giveaway sale prices, and he was wondering if his pocket money would stretch to one, and where he would hide it from his mother who preferred him to read improvingly, when suddenly he knew he was not alone. Reflected in the window was the tall narrow overcoat of Dirty Tex, topped by the long narrow face which glowed white like a half-moon against a shelf of dummy boxes of Black Magic. 'Our secret,' the voice already familiar from his nightmares breathed, and without turning to face the man, Nigel bolted home.

Several times in the next few weeks, and usually on his way home from school, he met Dirty Tex in the street. Always there was the coat and the gloves and the beret, sometimes an old-fashioned string shopping bag and always the pale, sickly face and the wet, dark-toothed smile. He never spoke again, but he would put his woolly finger to his lips and nod his head conspiratorially. The boy grew accustomed to this sporadic haunting, and found the man's live presence in many ways preferable to the suddenness and distortion of his appearance in nightmares. He began to feel that Dirty Tex would be about him for the rest of his life, smiling and abjuring silence on a secret that Nigel would never understand.

At times he suspected the secret had something to do with Tommy Fox's theory about how babies happened, a man and woman kissing and pressing together, but, if that were what the couple in the wood had been doing – and it seemed possible that it was – why would anyone watch them? And if they did, why would it be wrong? In any case, he hadn't been watching them. The confusion and unhappiness continued, made worse by the lack of anyone in whom he could safely confide. The fine days of early summer, which others seemed to be enjoying so much, seemed to him cold and dark.

And then in the first week of the school holiday another strange incident happened. His mother had two great comforts in her life of devotion and sacrifice. One was attending jumble sales and sales of work where she would acquire bargains which she took enormous pleasure in finding a use for. Like one of the minister's old shirts which she adapted to make a nightshirt for her son. At first Nigel had refused to wear it, but she had assured him that no one else would ever see it. If the doctor had to be called, Nigel would obviously wear his best pyjamas, and who else was there? He wondered how she could be sure that there would not be a fire one night, and he would have to be carried to safety down a ladder before crowds of laughing neighbours. But he gave in. And then there was the complete set of children's encyclopedias, thirty years old, the pages damp and curly, but only a pound for twelve volumes. And the kitchen chair which was all right if you didn't lean back. Nigel looked forward to these purchases with a mixture of curiosity and dread.

His mother's other hobby was finding those less fortunate than herself and winkling their stories from them. These were usually old men or women, of all ages, encountered on buses or in tearooms, approached with a casual remark about the weather and encouraged to tell the story of their lives. The object was not to find ways of helping these luckless victims of circumstance, because the conversations were firmly terminated when she got off the bus or paid for her tea, but to bring their sad tales back to her spotless home and recount them to her loving son, and feel a glow of contentment that she was not the spinster lonely after her mother's death or the man whose children in Australia never wrote to him or the old woman living in fear of her appointment with a specialist. 'I know I shouldn't say this, Nigel,' she would sigh, warming her hands at the fire, 'but I really ought to count my blessings.'

Now and then a neighbour's misfortune gave her a chance to show a more outgoing compassion, and she would take plates of soup and stew across the landing to the woman with her leg in plaster, or sit with the baby on the ground-floor right while his parents took a much needed night out. But her kindness never extended to inviting anyone into her home or her life, where there was only room for herself and her son. He was her only friend, and she wanted to be his.

She had the first Saturday in July off, so she took him to the bring-and-buy sale at the local church. As they stood outside in the queue, he could feel her sense of anticipation in the grip of her hand on his and, once inside, she handed over her three jars of home-made apple jelly, and took him on a brisk pre-opening tour of inspection. She pointed out what she meant to buy, the sweater that he would surely grow into in the next year, a hat which with a new trimming would go well with her winter coat and some cans of food which had lost their labels and were being offered at sixpence each.

A hush was called for the official opening by a famous singer of yesteryear, and she parked them both in front of the clothing stall, an arm's length away from the hat and the sweater. The speeches over, the applause had hardly died away before she had made her two purchases and was off in pursuit of the mystery cans. Nigel allowed the crowd to separate them so that he could make his way to the toy stall. These occasions had their own excitement for him: the crowds, the voices, the music, the sense of being dwarfed by everything but still, by reason of the coins in his pocket, to have power over the situation. The game was not to spend his money too quickly.

The toys turned out to be disappointing, jigsaw puzzles which would certainly be incomplete, a few battered cars, a sledge missing one runner and so many dolls and dolls' accessories that it seemed as if all the little girls in the district had abruptly grown up. He wandered towards the book stall, but here there was such a crowd that he had to wait till he could get close enough to browse, and it was as he waited that he caught sight of a familiar figure in an empty corner of the hall. Dirty Tex, wearing the same clothes as always but looking strangely confused and uncertain. It was the first time that Nigel had observed the man unnoticed, and he was surprised to see how pathetic he seemed, stooped and ridiculous, drained of all the menace that had disturbed Nigel over the past few weeks.

Not really understanding what he was doing, or why, the boy edged his way through the crowd until he stood a few feet from him. Now he could see the lost expression in the pink-rimmed eyes, and the way the gloved hands clenched and unclenched against the heavy material of the coat. The man seemed dazed by the noise and the people and had found the only place, near the emergency door, where he could feel apart from it all. Nigel was overwhelmed by a surge of pity for his enemy, and took a step forward so that Tex could not fail to see him.

At once the man became more alert, seemed to straighten and relax. He smiled and brought his finger up to his lips in the usual way. To Nigel's astonishment he found himself smiling back and nodding. They stood there for a moment, the man and the boy, in their quiet corner, smiling at each other, reassuring and reassured, and then Nigel became embarrassed and moved away, back to the book stall where he found a space free and still a fair selection to choose from.

But he could not concentrate. He lifted and laid musty-smelling books, but he hardly saw the titles. There was a pile of comics which he would normally have examined closely for issues he had missed, or for the kind of American comics forbidden by his mother for their violence, and therefore very intriguing. But he only flicked through the pile, aware of colour and texture, but no more.

Why had he done that? Deliberately gone to the man who had brought him so much fear and confusion, and demanded to be recognized. And when the man had smiled, he had smiled back! It was just something else to be puzzled and defeated by.

The woman serving at the stall made a little sound of reproof at the way Nigel was upsetting the neatness of the comics. As she leaned forward to tidy them, he looked up to apologise and saw behind her, in the narrow space reserved for helpers, Dirty Tex staring at him. As soon as he saw Nigel looking, his face lit up as if he were expecting they would exchange another friendly smile.

Nigel turned sharply away and pushed his way back to the toy stall. Its contents were depleted now, but a model plane had emerged from among the dolls' dresses. It looked well-used but still serviceable. A young man in Scout uniform was serving here. When Nigel went to ask him how much the plane was, he found Dirty Tex had sidled his way along the wall to stand behind the Scout. Again he tried a smile, but more tentatively this time, as if fearing another rejection. Nigel forgot about the plane and felt that it was important to find his mother, because this new haunting was more alarming than the old.

He fought his way to the canned food stall, but, of course, she was not there; nor were any of the unmarked tins. He searched up and down the two aisles of stalls, and all the time the man stayed level with him, ambling along between the stalls and the wall, unimpeded by anyone but those who were serving, and they were too preoccupied to give him more than an impatient glance. Now whenever he caught Nigel's eye, he winked at him and laughed. It was a game and the more Nigel ran, the more the man seemed to enjoy it, peek-a-booing at him round people's shoulders, waving and chortling to himself, apparently unaware that the boy was frightened.

It was another nightmare that Tex had pushed him into. Thudding against warm, solid bodies, squeezing between resistant coats and skirts and trousers, standing on toes, shoved this way and that . . . and his mother never in sight. It was like crawling backwards through the hawthorn again, but this time only one person was laughing at him, laughing the way a malicious playmate might, teasing him, unmoved by his increasing panic.

At last he noticed a door which he must have passed several times in the last few minutes. Above it was a roughly drawn sign reading 'Teas. Home-made Cakes and Scones'. Of course! Where else would she be? He barged in past those waiting and with immense relief saw her sitting at a table near the window. She waved and lifted her bag from the chair she had been keeping for him. He thought that perhaps now he ought to tell her about Dirty Tex. He was ready now for her comfort and support. She would know how to end this harassment.

But she was not alone. She had picked up a stout little woman with a red face, rimless glasses and a ring of white sausage curls round her head. She looked jollier, less put upon, than most of his mother's finds, and there were empty cups and the crumbs of a good few cakes and scones in front of them. Gratefully Nigel sat down. If Tex were watching – and he wasn't going to look round to make sure – he would see that the chase was over.

'This is my son,' his mother said proudly. 'Nigel, this is the lady who made that delicious tablet on the confectionery stall. Did you buy any?' Nigel said he hadn't. 'Never mind,' his mother said, 'I bought two bags which we can share later.'

The old woman leaned forward, her lively blue eyes enlarged by her spectacles. 'So what *have* you bought, sonny?' she asked kindly.

'Nothing yet,' he admitted.

His mother laughed, pleased. 'He's learned from me to be careful with money. We have to be, you know.'

'Oh, we're the same,' the old woman said. 'When I send Raymond out to the shops, I always give him a list and the right

39

money as near as I can reckon it. It's not easy, is it? You'd love to be able to say, "Spend what you want." '

Nigel's mother was about to say this was not one of her ambitions, that no matter how much money one had, one still had to be prudent with it, when the old woman glanced up and said, 'Ah, there's Raymond now.'

Nigel looked round, and there was the tall figure of Dirty Tex framed in the door of the tearoom. 'Oh, dear,' the old woman said, looking concerned, 'what's happened now?'

Tex's long face was even paler than Nigel had seen it, paper-white, and it was twisted into a mask of terror. His eyes stared wide and his mouth gaped. 'No!' he cried, and quickly the chatter in the tearoom faded.

'Oh, Raymond, pet! It's all right!' the old woman called to him and rose, her handbag tumbling unnoticed to the floor.

Tex's thunderstruck gaze was on Nigel, and he brought his finger – shakily, beseechingly – to his lips. Then he seemed to stiffen and grow taller before falling like a tree across one of the tables bringing it and its dishes down with him. There were cries of shock and sympathy, a few people moving to where he lay, more trying to get away from any involvement in an unseemly incident, and the old woman using her elbows to make a path between them and disappearing from sight.

Nigel rose and was about to stand on a chair to see what was going on, but his mother stopped him. 'What's wrong with him?' he asked, alarmed for his enemy.

'Fainted, I expect,' his mother said. She picked up the old woman's handbag, replaced the contents and clicked it shut. 'That poor woman. What she's had to put up with.'

She rose with the bag and her own shopper, and excused herself politely through the onlookers. Nigel followed, fearful of what he would see. The old woman and the man in Scout uniform were helping Tex – Raymond – into a chair. His face was still white, his eyelids flickering. He sagged limply on to the chair as if he had run a long distance, and his chin and the front of his coat were shiny with saliva. His beret had come off and among the black, wiry hair were bare patches of the same scaly skin as Nigel had seen on his face and wrists. The old woman whispered soothingly as she wiped his mouth and chin with her handkerchief. When a waitress brought a glass of water, she gave her a calm, grateful smile, as if this were something that had happened before, and the kindness of strangers was what she expected.

Nigel hung back, afraid the man would see him and cry out or collapse again, because this was one incident he did understand. He knew exactly why Raymond had been taken ill. The man sipped from the tumbler held by his mother and began to look around him. Almost at once he saw Nigel, and his face crumpled as if he were about to cry. Quickly, and out of sight of the two mothers, Nigel raised his finger to his lips and nodded. He wanted to add a reassuring smile, but none would come. Urgently he repeated his message of secrecy and trust, and saw the man relax, and becoming aware of himself as the centre of a scene, begin to resist his mother's attentions, his face sullen and closed as he tried to dodge the offered glass and the dabs of the hankie.

Nigel's mother laid the handbag at the old woman's side, and said quietly and firmly, 'You'll manage now, my dear, won't you?' Without waiting for an answer she led Nigel away.

Later as they sat at the kitchen table sampling the old woman's tablet, she told him, 'Poor soul, she has had terrible problems with him ever since he was born and he's thirty-three now. He has these allergies, you see, things he can't eat or even be in contact with. His skin is affected and he feels the cold in all weathers. And he has asthma. We really should count our blessings, you know.' She passed the paper bag across the table. 'Have another piece. It's delicious, isn't it!'

In truth Nigel found it too sweet, and was put off by its association with what had happened at the sale. 'I've had enough,' he said.

'Good boy,' she said approvingly, and closed the bag. 'I'll make the tea in a minute.' She grew thoughtful again. Her chewing slowed as she seemed to find something very deep to ponder on. 'Strange,' she said at last, dreamily. 'He's like a child really. He'll always need her, always be dependent on her. As long as he lives, she will always have her son to look after. He'll never leave her.'

He was aware of her eyes on him and grew uncomfortable. Her expression sharpened as she looked at him. 'You know,' she said, 'I could have sworn it was you he was staring at just before he collapsed. Have you ever seen him before?'

'No', he said, looking surprised by the question. He remembered how close he had been to telling her everything about the incident in the Bluebell Wood and the subsequent haunting, and he found himself thinking that he must never again tell her anything that might make him appear weak. The thought saddened him. 'No, I would have remembered if I'd seen somebody like that before.'

She seemed satisfied, and got up to put the kettle on. 'Set the table, please, Nigel.'

As he took the tablecloth from the drawer, he asked, 'Can I go out to play after tea?'

'For an hour or so,' she said, lighting the gas. 'In the park, of course.'

'Yes,' he said, thinking of the clearing by the convent wall and of mysteries unsolved. 'In the park.'

FRIDAY'S CHILD

Moira Burgess

'Ah, shut yer face, Robbie,' she said, and hugged him, her voice breaking on an excited laugh. The squirming two-year-old peered up through his eyelashes, as surprised as herself, and she got a suspicious glare from a fat woman in a headscarf brushing heavily past. No wonder, giggling in the street in the middle of a Monday morning, outside the doctor's too. She bit the back of her hand and swallowed down the unbelieving bubbling joy.

The baby was whining in his pram. She heaved the little boy on to his seat, kicked back the brake, and leaned to the hill. 'Sooner push a pair o' elephants,' she said to them, out of habit. The dragging ache started up low in her back, but she could stand it, she could stand anything now. Ahead of her the steep street met in a firm thin line the plunging sky. It would be like that, a sharp edge, an end. She clucked to the baby and sang to the little boy and jolted the heavy pram on and off the broken high kerbs. Black sadness waited just beyond her busy thoughts, but that she pushed away.

The shops were not too crowded, and the girls seemed unusually kind: she smiled back at them, feeling like a bride. God, some bride! Sausages, cough-bottle, potatoes, library books for Jimmy. The pram was loaded; she stopped for a moment to clear her head. One good push more, and then over the crest, and ah, the peace, the quiet mind. She pushed, and the easy time began.

The grey street was long, but it was flat. They would even get out of this, in the smooth days ahead; time to plan, a chance to save some money. The big loose wheels whispered over greasy chip-papers and dogs' dirt. Rocked to peace, the baby stopped girning and blinked his kitten eyes. The sadness came from behind, all unexpected, and threw her down. Would it be there a year from now, laying its cold hand on her belly whenever she saw a pregnant wife? But few women got this chance; she was the lucky one, looking at the latest baby and knowing that he was the last.

'Ah, son,' she said to the baby, who beamed with his toothless mouth. But her head was swimming now, cold sweat breaking under her arms; she stopped again and leaned on the handle of the pram. No, it would be worth it, worth anything, after eight years, to feel well again. Your body could get tired out, nobody's fault: 'Phone as soon as you like,' the doctor had said, 'I'll get the arrangements under way.' She smiled sadly at the baby, seeing an empty pram.

The high peeling hall was dark, and from the basement the three-year-old's screams shook and sobbed. She shut the front door as quietly as she could, but it rattled in its warped frame, and Miss Fernie didn't need as much warning as that.

'There's not anything wrong with the wee girl, is there, Mrs Clark? That's an awful din she's making.'

'No, no, Miss Fernie, thanks for asking though.' Yellow fingers fidgeting at the pocked varnish: she was never done getting on to Robbie for marking her door, but Jimmy swore she did it herself when she ran out of blackheads. 'She's had a wee bit of a cold again, I think that's it.'

'Nothing infectious, I hope.'

'No, nothing like that, sorry to disappoint you.' Now she really was going daft, often as she'd wanted to say that to the old bitch; but Miss Fernie with a long thin sniff had already faded back into her twilit room. The three-year-old howled and roared. She braked the pram roughly beside the phone-box and thudded down the stone stair. The child sat weeping on the bottom step. In their room, over a grey fire, Jimmy was reading. This week he was thinking of becoming a geologist.

'What's the matter wi' Flora?' she said, wiping the little girl's dirty face.

'Damn all,' he said. 'She's never stopped since ye've went oot. Did ye get my books?'

'Oh aye,' she said, 'they're upstairs.' She went up to the hall, unstrapped and hauled out the complaining children, and carried them downstairs one by one.

She had left the books in the hall. Jimmy's black brows went down, but he didn't say anything. He reached out for Robbie and held him between his knees. The wee boy was the dark one, curly black hair and black eyes, a heartbreaker some day. Trapped, cross, in the circle of his father's strength, he reflected sulkily the handsome dark face above him.

'Where's wee Jean?' she said.

'Where d'ye think?' he said, winding his arms round the boy and rocking him to and fro.

She filled the kettle at the sink, looking out over the square grey back court. In its far corner wee Jean, wet-nosed with the cold that had kept her off school, was playing at houses with the toddler from next door. As she watched, wee Ethel's dirty hand dug into her thin dark hair in a long satisfying claw. God, the fine-tooth comb again tonight; but you couldn't blame wee Ethel. What kind of a chance did she get? You would wonder how Jimmy could sleep so sound some nights, with the thuds and screams coming through the wall.

Passing behind his chair to get to the gas cooker, she ran her hand over the tight curls that capped his head, just like Robbie's.

'What was that for?' he said with a yawn.

'Oh nothin',' she said. 'You never knock me about anyway.'

'To hell,' he said. He was so astonished that she began to giggle. 'Here, hold on a minute! What d'ye mean, *anyway*?'

'Oh, God,' she said, wiping her eyes. 'Nothin'. I'm daft the day.' She set the kettle on the old green stove and lit it with the usual bang and the seeping smell of gas. 'I wis at the doctor's,' she said.

'Oh aye,' he said, 'an' how are you?'

'No' too bad.' After a moment or two she said, 'No' too good

45

neither,' but she had left it too long. He wasn't listening. He bent his head to Robbie's black curls and said 'Who's his daddy's wee man?' The little boy squirmed and kicked. 'G'wan then ye wee bugger,' the man said, and let him go.

'We talked a good bit.'

'Who?' he said crossly.

'Me an' the doctor. I think,' she said, turning away from him, 'she wanted to find out what religion we were.'

'She's got a good cheek then. Here!' he said. 'She's no' one herself, is she?'

'Naw, naw,' she said. 'Only –' She picked up the baby and took him to the sink. The tiredness was catching her now under the heart. 'Only she says I shouldny have very many more weans.' She unpinned the nappy, folding it away from the red little legs. 'No' any more,' she said, 'in fact.'

He slewed round and looked at her under his brows like a young bull.

'You know what *like I am*,' she said apologetically. 'You've only to look at me an' I've fell pregnant again.'

'Aw here,' he said, 'I dae more'n look surely?' He reached out and smacked her bottom. Robbie and the little girl screamed with laughter and ran over to beat a tattoo on her skirt with hard little fists.

'Ah, Robbie, Flora, stop it now,' she said. Her back was very sore. 'Only that's been eight years –'

She could see insult gathering dark on his handsome brow. 'Ye were keen enough once,' he said. 'I suppose ye wish ye were back wi' your faither.'

'Oh, Jimmy, I didny say that,' she said. 'I wouldny wish that.' The thin tough old man sucking his tea at the bare table: sucking her life away, Jimmy had said. She had turned twenty-seven in the damp dark house, twenty-eight, twenty-nine, like the tick of the dusty marble clock, till Mrs Dane across the landing got a new young lodger. Jimmy had been thinking of becoming a poet at that time, but then he had been in a job at least.

'It wis my lucky day, the day I met you,' she said. She wiped

46

and dried and shook talcum powder, not looking up. 'Only my mammy had me when she was forty-five. I could go on ten year yet. An' that's seven times already, ye see.'

'Countin' the misses,' he said impatiently.

She was silent for a moment, but he didn't seem to think he had said anything out of the way. How would he, a man? 'She asked me about the pill,' she said, 'but I had to say I didny think I could keep it up. An' the jag, I'm no' keen on that.'

'Just as bloody well,' he said. 'I told ye afore, I'm no' goin' tae bed wi' some kinna dustbin.'

'But she says we've tae –' That was a wrong word, she could tell already. 'She thinks we should dae somethin' aboot it.'

'Did ye no' tell her we tried?'

'I did,' she said, 'an' she asked where the last yin came from.'

'Be damned her bloody cheek,' he said. 'D'ye no' mind it wis the New Year?'

'I know,' she said, 'ye couldny help it.' She turned and looked down at his smooth broad back in the white shirt, his proud curly head, the strong blunt line of his jaw and chin. She stirred and moved. 'So then there's the next thing. I could go intae hospital an' get tied. Then, ye see, I couldny have any more.'

'Tied?' he said.

'That's what they ca' it.' Now it was out, her breath came easier. 'It's a kinna wee operation, that's all. They asked me right enough when I wis in havin' him,' she said, folding and refolding the clean napkin, 'only I wis – It a' seems better when ye're just bye. I thought we might be okay this time.'

He turned round in his chair to stare at her. 'An' are we no'?' he said.

She had come out with the wrong thing again. She said soothingly, 'I didny mean that, Jimmy. Only my monthlies is back an' we're still – You're no' –'

'I telt ye it's no' the same usin' them!'

'This way ye wouldny need to!' she cried. But he had turned away again; he hunched over, elbows on knees, and stuck out his lip, and picked at a ragged nail. She found she had the napkin wrung hard as a hawser in her hands. 'Anyway I said

I'd phone her back,' she said. 'I said I couldny say yes withoot tellin' – withoot askin' you.'

She waited, watching him. She nearly began to think he hadn't heard. She looked at his long-fingered hands, and wondered if she would say it again.

'An operation,' he said. 'Hell o' a risk that.'

'It's no' dangerous,' she said eagerly. 'They do it day an' daily.'

'A' the same.' He shook his head deeply like a soothsayer. 'An operation. I couldny take it on myself, hen. I couldny put ye through that.'

She waited and waited, because it had to dawn on him: but it didn't, and it wasn't going to. 'But Jimmy,' she said, 'the thing is –' Ah God, where did you begin?

He said over his shoulder, sounding hurt, 'I thought ye wis fond o' the weans.'

In the backwash of that pain she found herself saying, 'Jimmy –'

'Aye?'

'It disny make any difference tae – tae –'

'Aye, whit?'

'You know,' she said, almost voiceless. 'Whit ye were sayin' there. Sex an' that.'

He flung himself round so that the chair nearly tipped over. 'Who says?' he snarled.

'The doctor –'

He stared at her, breathing fast, dark-red in the face. 'She's a bloody wumman,' he said.

The ache in her back was so bad she wanted to be sick. But the baby was kicking on the draining-board; she smoothed out the twisted napkin and caught the cushiony ankles between her fingers. She said, 'So that's a' aboot it then.'

'Whit kinna life's that for me,' he said sulkily, 'half a bloody man?'

'It's no' like that –' She put her head down and pinned the nappy on the wriggling baby. 'So I've tae phone the doctor,' she said, 'whether or no'.'

'Aye, well,' he said.

Up in the hall, with the baby on her shoulder, it took her a minute or two to dial the number. As it rang, Jimmy came thumping upstairs through the baize door. She waited for him to speak, her clenched hand with the receiver in it pressed over her heart. With a scowl he picked up her forgotten shopping-bag and found his library books. He examined them, nodding darkly.

'Naw,' he said, 'if you went intae hospital who would look after the weans?'

He clattered away downstairs as the pips began at the other end. She pressed the money into the slot. 'Doctor?' she said. 'Aye, it is.' She listened to the voice for a few moments. 'No,' she said, 'I've changed my mind.'

The doctor was still speaking when she put the receiver down. The baby jumped in her arms and pain stabbed through and through her back and loins. 'Ah ye wee bastard,' she said, and shook him as hard as she could, her fingers gripping bruisingly in his fat little shoulder.

PAGES FROM A LIFE

Felicity Carver

It's there in the cupboard. A brown bottle with a pure white tuft of cotton wool stopping the orifice, enclosing sleep like the evil jinn in an Eastern tale. If I had the strength to reach it.

I do.

But I don't use it.

There is an egg on my breakfast tray, a brilliant orange yolk pouring over the rim of the shell. I never did like eggs, but the nurse always brings one each morning, talking cosily as if to a child. 'We will eat it today, won't we?' My sister Camilla used to make a hole in the base of the egg, allowing the yolk and watery white to run into the egg-cup so that she wouldn't have to eat it; no one ever noticed, but she could have talked and smiled her way out of trouble anyhow, she had the ability to make others look awkward and ungracious by comparison.

The nurse has come in again. I can't remember her name now; yesterday it was with me all the time. She will help me dress and shave, take charge of me, make me presentable as she would with a baby. I try to talk to her, but since the illness my speech is unclear, my tongue does not always form the words I look for, fricatives hiss and trip on the teeth that don't fit too well. Like others she assumes a lack of speech means lack of intelligence. I understand though; she reminds me of the governess Camilla and I shared, who had too much knowledge for her experience. We saw my cousin Tom kiss Miss Winter the day before his leave expired; watching through the banisters we saw him place his arm round her waist, they swayed backwards and forwards, their faces together, while Camilla's nails dug into my arm and the wrought iron rails barred my view. Then his hands must have strayed too far, she broke away, affronted, and spent the afternoon in her room, not coming down to tea because of a headache. We knew from her eyes she had been crying; perhaps she was upset at her refusal. This one who comes to take away my tray would be the same.

There is another nurse who comes at night; she is used to men, she handles my impotence with ease, nothing surprises her, she does not talk to cover embarrassment. Quick with slang and swearing, alive and cheerful, surely she has other things to do with her nights, not looking after old men.

So Catto is here today. I have her name again. A Scot, with cold blue eyes, the sandy hair and freckled skin of Scandinavian ancestry. She picks clothes out of my wardrobe, taking them like costumes for a doll. Buttoning my cuffs for me because my hand does not function too well any more; I manage the pullover more easily.

'Is it cold?'

She understands this time. 'No, a lovely mild spring day, do you good to go out.'

She is tying my laces for me; the leather is pulled tight over the instep. I feel as if I can pick up my childhood with my good hand, it is close, vivid, something to return to. When we move into the hall Catto's professional arm is at my elbow to steady me in case the rug has curled and is lying in wait for shuffling feet. My coat is thick and warm like a blanket; I cannot sit outside without it, my feet and hands grow numb, the circulation is poor. Miss Winter is buttoning up the top button of my velvet-collared coat, we are going out to see something special, we have been good, she will take us to the botanical gardens, an educational treat. They always wear uniforms. Miss Winter's was of her own design, dresses in a suitable hard-wearing grey with soft white collars; Catto wears an overall, blue and white. I tell her to wear her own clothes but she prefers to keep the identity of an institution, she is frightened of being herself. I try and explain this to her, but she won't listen, she handles me out of the front door with brisk fearfulness, we walk along the pavement to the strip of gardens and trees which she calls the park. I can walk on my own once I am across the road, I am free to sense the spring in the shouts of the children and the barking of dogs, to watch the blur of bright greens and moving leaves. There is a seat here; my weight folds onto it, I am anchored to the slatted boards, it will be an effort to rise again.

I wait for the girl to come. I do not know her name, but she reminds me of Camilla. Not that they are alike to look at: Camilla was fair and graceful with a natural charm, whereas this girl is dark and small and wild, full of defiance and suspicion. She leads the boys, she is the first to climb the tree beside the seat, to drop off the swing at the top of its arc, landing and scrabbling for her balance on the worn grass; she is afraid sometimes, but like Camilla she does not want anyone to know. When we went to the Prescotts Camilla was also frightened of the dog, but she did not run as I did, she stood still as we had been told and used her voice to make friends with the animal which stood on the steps, hackles forming a fin on its back, rumbling deep in its throat. 'I'll tell them to keep it in next time we come,' she said. They did what she wanted, as everyone did. Camilla was my protector; with her calm clear gaze, confident and poised, she could talk to adults on their own terms, she had no problems with Miss Winter, apart from the one occasion.

This girl laughs at me together with the other children; they play a kind of grandmother's footsteps sometimes, creeping up to the seat, trying to see if I have noticed them. Once I felt someone touch my back, but when I turned around they had gone and there was only laughter echoing from the bushes. I don't mind their ridicule; perhaps inside them something is afraid of age and ugliness and growing old, they do not understand yet. Yesterday she came and stood in front of me, a child who seems half-boy, half-girl, insolent and graceful, thick lashes curving over the round dark eyes.

'Hey Mister, got anything for us?'

I shook my head; my speech might have scared her.

She hesitated, moving her weight from one foot to the other, ready to run if I did something she didn't like. Perhaps the question was a dare. She was dressed as usual in a grubby shirt, jeans that had probably belonged to someone else first; an open face with a smile that shows a missing tooth, brown hair that falls forward into her eyes. Then one of the others called and she ran off, an uneven skipping stride.

'Can you get me some sweets?'

I asked the nurse who comes at night. Catto would want to know why, would talk about teeth and create difficulties.

'Sure,' she said, dark-skinned hands smoothing the sheets. 'What kinds?'

'Something children would like.'

'Expecting visitors?' My great-nephews are too old for sweets, but she is new, she does not know that.

'Yes.' When she brings them, I will put them in my coat pocket when Catto is out of the way, preparing a meal in the kitchen, cutting thin bread and butter because she thinks that is the correct way to have it.

This morning they were painting white lines on the road; they shine in the sunlight, a rubberized strip of white, antiseptic as surgical tape.

That day was full of lines. On the table in the schoolroom there were grooves carved in the surface; if you sharpened your pencil and dug it into the soft wood, it would make railway tracks, tramlines, channels that reached the edge of the flat world of the table and fell off into space. There were lines on the pages of the atlas forming borders round coloured countries; some of them remain forever yellow and green in my mind.

'What is the equator?'

'It's a line round the middle of the earth.' I knew it, I felt successful, I had thwarted Miss Winter's attempt to find something I didn't know.

'No, that's wrong!' She had been trying to persuade my parents that I should go away to school soon, I had heard them in the dining room after breakfast, discussing when I should go. 'His health, he's too young,' my mother had said, and Miss Winter had come out looking irritated. She would have preferred teaching Camilla alone; they did everything for the first time, it was new and interesting, whereas my turn was repetition. Also I was not interested in physical pursuits, I liked music and drawing; she told tales of her previous charges, she had admired their wildness, she called them 'real boys'. I was not sure I qualified.

'But it is a line.'

'No, an *imaginary* line.' Triumphant stress on the word.

'It can't be an imaginary line. It's there, look.' I was kind, I pointed it out on the page, a thin dark line with 'Equator O°' written in small italic print above it.

'Dear child, surely you don't think there is a line drawn on the earth to mark it, do you?'

'But why do they show it if it isn't there?'

'Because it's the Equator.'

'But if it's imaginary it shouldn't be on the atlas?'

'Of course you have to know where it is. In order to navigate.'

It looked as solid as the lines for canals, railways or boundaries; I could not believe that somewhere on the earth there was not a line or mark showing that this was the middle of the world. How else would anyone know it was there?

In an afternoon of brilliant sunlight I had to stay in, to write out Miss Winter's definition of the Equator; more lines, of sprawling writing on the feint blue lines of the paper, letters scraped with a nib that split if pressed too hard, ink that ran and flooded suddenly. Outside I could hear Camilla and a friend, another girl, in the garden; four years older, they had different games, other secrets from which I was sometimes excluded. There was a heavy scent of flowers in the air from the herbaceous border below the window, roses shedding petals on the dry ground. The lines on the paper merged, the nib split finally and traced double lines on the page, and I finished and looked around for amusement, not certain if I was allowed to leave.

The cuckoo clock in the corner ticked incessantly, the pendulum swaying, some arrangement of leaves carved in dark wood. It belonged to Miss Winter; one of her first actions on arrival had been to put it up, to let us know that we too were amongst the privileged few who were allowed to have Miss Winter's clock in our schoolroom. Not just a clock, but a cuckoo clock all the way from Switzerland. We had the impression that some-one who was important in her life had given it to her; Camilla made up stories about him, a student who was too poor to marry her, but had bought her the clock as a present before he died of consumption. She wrote stories about heroes who were all poets and died of consumption, and read them to me on dull afternoons when the house was quiet.

It was a few minutes to the hour. I did something I had always wanted to do, and pulled a chair across the floor to the clock. Standing on the chair, I would be able to see the cuckoo better when it came out; a blue and white bird that plunged through the small door and jerked out the broken notes of its monotonous song; there was a fascination about its swift movement and the impossibility of stopping it. The heavy weights, shaped like fircones, swung at the end of chains; the clock was wound by a ceremonial pulling on these cones, they made a noise like material being ripped. I heard the familiar buzz of the spring which always came just before the bird appeared; the small door swung open and the bird flew out, wheezing. I caught hold of it but the spring was too strong, my fingers hit the door and a nail tore a little, the bird retreated into wooden silence and I heard Miss Winter's voice in anger from the door. I was treated to a lecture as she inspected the damage; her irritation was suffocating.

Towards evening, the sky grew dark with thunderclouds and Camilla and I ran in excitement through the house and garden, uneasy at the distant rumbling, calling out to each other in the humid air, waiting for the rain to fall and freshen the dusty flowers. The oppressive sky made everyone uncomfortable, my mother retreated with a headache, Miss Winter was still angry, and I went to bed feeling as if it was not the end of the day, or not the way it ought to end.

The thunder woke me, or perhaps it was the lightning first, a flash that lit the walls of my room, and a sudden clap like gunfire, or a plane breaking the sound barrier, though that wasn't something I had heard then. It went on, the sky fought above the house and a branch fell from the cedar tree, and I was frightened by the noise and went through to Camilla's room, my feet cold and silent on the boards in the passage. She was lying awake, her long hair brushed out, streaming on the pillow.

'Isn't it marvellous,' she said. 'It's so bright.' Lightning lit the room briefly; we counted the seconds until the sky exploded outside, and I sat on the bed shivering as I listened.

'Here.' She turned back the sheets and moved over to one side, I crept into the warmth where she had been lying, and we curled up, back to back, Camilla staring at the window, until the rain fell and hammered on the roof of the porch below and the night was full of the sound of water and I fell asleep.

Miss Winter must have found us like that; I suppose she had remembered that I was frightened of thunder and had gone to find my room empty. I was aware of being shaken roughly, of Camilla saying, 'It doesn't matter, he was safe here, I thought it best.' I was hustled back to my room, to the rumpled bed, and the smell of fresh damp earth came through the open window where a pool of rain had collected on the sill.

They talked in quiet voices next day, conversations from which I was excluded. I was aware of having apparently done something wrong, but no one would tell me what it was. I hovered outside doors, hoping to catch an explanation as I had hoped to catch the bird in the clock, but it was equally futile. Camilla was angry, but would not confide.

'We think it may be time for you to go away to school after all.'

'You're about the right age,' said Miss Winter. 'You'll enjoy the company of other boys, the cricket and football. Being in the company of girls all the time isn't right, really.' She was smiling a little; it didn't fit with my mother's expression, she looked thoughtful, serious, but did not say much.

It was a long time before I realized what it was all about, but it didn't alter the effect of leaving home, of leaving Camilla. I didn't understand at first that she would not be going away as well. Miss Winter had separated us, we grew away from each other after that. I became able at least to act the part of a real boy in a way Miss Winter would have liked; I went to boarding-school and afterwards to Oxford, and while I was there Camilla, who had married an American, died while her second child was born, some unexpected complication.

I can remember that so clearly now; I was afraid I wouldn't be able to write it down. Sometimes my mind picks up the wrong ends of things, fumbles with memories and fails to disentangle them. It is all there, though: thunder is inextricably mixed with the warmth of Camilla and the feeling of an unexplained misdemeanour, a guilt that others carried for me, an importance attached to something that seemed trivial to both of us.

Today in the gardens I gave the girl the sweets. She came up again, speculatively, an animal still half wild. She wouldn't take them from my dry lizard-skin hand, but when my fingers failed to hold them she stooped and picked them up swiftly, then moved away back to her friends in the safety of the trees. But they are not nervous now: I am a possible source of something good, they don't play behind my back so much.

I think Catto has her suspicions that I am writing something. I pretend it is a letter, but she keeps asking if I need stamps, and I have to say that I haven't finished yet. 'A long letter,' she commented yesterday. I keep the pages in a book of poetry I have by my bed; she is not interested in reading, it will be a safe place. I do not want her to see this, I dislike the thought of her ignorance misinterpreting things she could not understand.

The night nurse did not come last night; I wasn't able to arrange to buy more sweets. Tubes of bright colours, strange gifts, like beads for natives. Jackson took me out this morning, and I borrowed some change off him. Everyone looks after my needs here, they do not expect me to have common wants, I am like some over-protected prince in a fairy tale, all the things I need are supplied. The physical things. Except for the ability to move easily and speak swiftly. I am the nucleus of a small group, everything revolves round what I want. Or seems to. There are other worlds though, for instance that of Jackson and

Catto. They had an argument yesterday, I could not hear what was said but the tones were clear, then Catto came upstairs, flushed by his linguistic assault, on edge and ruffled like a startled hen. When she is angry, her hands are rough, she does not realize it.

I offered the girl money this morning, a few coins in a gloved palm, a hand that shakes a little. She hesitated again, then yelled to her friends. 'See, here!' They come over as well, small figures with similar features, perhaps they are mostly one family. 'Thanks.' A sudden flash of white teeth, the gap still there, and they scatter and run and gather round the swing. The sun feels warmer when they are there; I forget the edges of the seat pressing through coat and trousers, the numbness in my feet disappears in their cries and the colour of their motley clothes. I am buying friendship, I know, but I can't take the money with me. What else do I have to offer? If I could speak more clearly, I could talk to them, tell them things, but they would possibly think my stories were ridiculous and old-fashioned. Not even friendship, just association, being allowed to watch their squabbles and scuffles, the cries from one rejected, the adults who come occasionally and deal out rough justice amongst the group, protecting their own.

'He was giving her money.'

I heard them again, in the kitchen. I have my lunch in the sitting room when the weather is mild, the sun comes through the window and floods the far end.

'At his age!'

'She came round, really upset she was. Said he'd got to stay away.'

'Free country.'

'That's what I said. If she's worried, then she can keep her little girl away. Said she was going to.'

'Do they really think?'

They will separate us with innuendo, with conversations behind half-closed doors. I will be sent away again; they did it once, a long time ago, it could happen again. I cannot let them do that, not now. I need the warmth, the boards are cold under my feet, the bottle is on the side, all I have to do is raise myself and walk over to it.

The scent of rain is coming through the window.

Jackson heard the thud while he ate his lunch; Catto and he exchanged glances, then Jackson hurried through the hall, flinging the sitting room door wide. He wasn't sure what he expected until he saw the figure on the floor, an untidy heap of clothes, the dull humped form, a shadow across the sunlight.

'Here,' he said, reluctant to accept responsibility.

'Leave him to me.' Catto was official in dark blue.

'Is he . . .?' Jackson didn't want to finish the sentence, to make it final. Catto put her head down to the grey face, listened a moment. The lips moved a little. 'Help me lift him, I don't think anything's broken. And then ring the doctor.'

The words formed kaleidoscopic patterns in his mind, breaking and swirling away; she sensed his desperation to communicate from where he lay on the wide sofa. 'Into?' she said encouragingly, picking up a sound. 'Winter? No dear, it's summer, well spring anyway, not winter.' He was being fobbed off again, he strained at the cushions, trying to raise his head, and the small table beside the sofa overturned and a book of verse fell onto the floor. Catto caught him, surprised at his strength, then he relaxed, slipped back on the cushions.

'I've rung,' said Jackson, nervous at the door.

Catto's fingers were a divining rod on the thin wrist. Jackson picked up the book, and sheets of closely written paper fell from the pages.

'What's all this?'

He showed her the writing. 'Here,' he said. 'It doesn't make sense. He's got some of the words right, but the rest is just scribbles.'

'He said he was writing letters. Seemed to give him pleasure, poor thing, so I just let him have the paper.'

'Wonder what he thought he was writing.' He glanced at the figure on the sofa. Catto did not let him ask, enjoying the power the knowledge gave her. Instead she smoothed her overall and walked over to the window, flinging it wide open, feeling the warm spring air on her face, listening to the voices of children playing in the park.

THE OLD WOMAN, THE BABY AND TERRY

Iain Crichton Smith

The fact was that the old woman wanted to live. All her faculties, her energies, were shrunken down to that desire. She drew everything into herself so that she could live, survive. It was obscene, it was a naked obscenity.

'Do you know what she's doing now?' said Harry to his wife Eileen. 'She keeps every cent. She hoards her pension, she's taken to hiding her money in the pillow slips, under blankets. She reminds me of someone, I can't think who.'

'But what can we do?' said Eileen who was expecting a baby.

Harry worked with a youth organization. He earned £7000 a year. There was one member of the organization called Terry MacCallum who, he thought, was insane. Terry had tried to rape one of the girls on the snooker table one night. He was a psychopath. Yet Harry wanted to save him. He hated it when he felt that a case was hopeless.

'She won't even pay for a newspaper,' said Harry.

'I know,' said Eileen. 'This morning I found her taking the cigarette stubs from the bucket.'

The child jumped in her womb. She loved Harry more than ever: he was patient and kind. But he grew paler every day: his work was so demanding and Terry MacCallum was so mad and selfish.

'I've never met anyone like him,' said Harry. 'His selfishness is a talent, a genius. It's diamond hard, it shines. I should get rid of him, I know that. Also he's drunk a lot of the time. He said to me yesterday, I don't care for anyone. I'm a bastard, you know that. I'm a scrounger, I hate everyone.'

Harry couldn't understand Terry. Everything that was done for him he accepted and then kicked you in the teeth. He was a monster. He haunted his dreams.

The child kicked in Eileen's womb. She wanted it badly. She had a hunger for it. She wanted it to suck her breasts, she wanted it to crawl about the room, she wanted it to make her alive again.

And all the time the old lady hoarded her banknotes. Eileen mentioned to her that they needed bread but she ignored hints of any kind. She even hoarded the bread down the sides of her chair. She tried to borrow money from Eileen. She sang to herself. She gathered her arms around herself, she was like a plant that wouldn't die. Eileen shuddered when she looked at her. She thought that she was sucking her life from her but not like the baby. The baby thrived, it milked her, it grew and grew. She was like a balloon, she thrust herself forward like a ship. The baby was like a ship's prow.

'I tried talking to him,' said Harry. 'I can't talk to him at all. He doesn't understand. I can't communicate. He admits everything, he thinks that the world should look after him. He wants everything, he has never grown up. I have never in my life met such selfishness. If he feels sexy he thinks that a woman should put out for him immediately. If he feels hungry he thinks that other people should feed him. I am kind to him but he hates me. What can you do with those who don't see? Is there a penance for people like that? What do you do with those who can't understand?'

The baby moved blindly in her womb, instinctively, strategically. She said to Harry, 'I'm frightened. Today I thought that the ferns were gathering round the house, that they wanted to eat me. I think we should cut the ferns down.' 'Not in your condition,' said Harry. He looked thin, besieged.

The old lady said, 'I don't know why you married him. He doesn't make much money, does he? Why doesn't he move to the city? He could make more money there.' She hid a teabag in her purse. And a biscuit.

The child moved in the womb. It was a single mouth that sucked. Blood, milk, it sucked. It grew to be like its mother. It sang a song of pure selfishness. It had stalks like fern. The stars at night sucked dew from the earth. The sun dried the soil. Harry had the beak of a seagull.

'Last night he wouldn't get off the snooker table,' said Harry. 'There are others who want to play, I said to him. This is my snooker table, he said. It isn't, I said. It is, he said. You try and take it off me. And then he said, Lend me five pounds. No, I said. Why, he said. Because you're selfish, I said. I'm not, he said. I'm a nice fellow, everyone says so. I've got a great sense of humour. What do you do with someone like that? I can't get through to him at all. And yet I must.'

'What for?' said Eileen.

'I just have to.'

'You never will.'

'Why not?'

'Just because. Nature is like that. I don't want the child.'

'What?'

'I know what I mean. Nature is like that. I don't want the child.'

Harry had nightmares. He was on an operating table. A doctor was introducing leeches into his veins. The operating table was actually for playing snooker on. It had a green velvet surface. He played with a baby's small head for a ball.

The ferns closed in. In the ferns she might find pound notes. She began to eat bits of coal, stones, crusts. She gnawed at them hungrily. The old lady wouldn't sleep at night. She took to locking her door. What if something happened? They would have to break the door down.

The baby sucked and sucked. Its strategies were imperative. It was like a bee sucking at a flower with frantic hairy legs, its head buried in the blossom, its legs working.

Terry stole some money after the disco. He insisted it was his.

'You lied to me,' said Harry.

'I didn't lie.'

'You said you were at home. I 'phoned your parents. They said you were out. You lied to me.'

'I didn't lie.'

'But can't you see you said one thing and it wasn't the truth. Can you not see that you lied?'

'I didn't lie.'

'For Christ's sake are you mad? You did lie. What do you think a lie is? Can't you see it?'

'I didn't lie.'

'You'll have to go.'

The old lady had a pile of tea bags, quarter pounds of butter, cheese, in a bag under the bed.

'You owe me,' she said to Eileen. 'For all those years you owe me. I saw it in the paper today that it takes ten thousand pounds to rear a child. You owe me ten thousand pounds. It said that in the paper.'

'You haven't paid for that paper,' said Eileen. 'I've tried my best, don't you understand? How can you be so thick?'

'You owe me ten thousand pounds,' said the old lady in the same monotonous grudging voice. 'It said in the paper. I read it.'

'You are taking my beauty away from me,' said Eileen to the baby. 'You are sucking me dry. You are a leech. You are Dracula. You have blood on your lips. And you don't care.'

She carried the globe in front of her. It had teeth painted all over it.

Harry became thinner and thinner. I must make Terry understand, he kept saying. He must be made to understand, he has
never in his whole life given anything to anyone. I won't let him
go till I have made him understand. It would be too easy to get
rid of him.

Put him out, said Eileen, abort him.

What did you say?

Abort him.

You said abort. I'm frightened.

'Can't you see,' said Eileen. 'That's what it is. People feed and
feed. Cows feed on grass, grass feeds on bones, bones feed on
other bones. It's a system. The whole world is like a mouth.
Blake was wrong. It's not a green and pleasant land at all. The
rivers are mouths. The sun is the biggest mouth of all.'

'Are you all right, Eileen?'

'Oh hold me,' said Eileen.

And they clung together in the night. But Eileen said, 'Look
at the ceiling. Do you see it? It's a spider.' It hung like a black
pendant. A moth swam towards the light from the darkness
outside. The spider was a patient engineer. Suddenly Eileen
stood on top of the bed and ripped the web apart. Bastard, she
said. Go and find something else to do. The spider had chubby
fists. It was a motheaten pendant.

Terry the psychopath smiled and smiled. He bubbled with
laughter. 'Give me,' he said to his mother, 'ten pounds of my
birthday money in advance.'

'No.'

'Why not? You were going to give it to me anyway.'

'And what are you going to give me for my birthday?'

'I'll think of something.'

'You won't give me anything, will you? Not a thing will you
give me.'

The old woman stole sausages from the fridge, matches from
the cupboard. She borrowed cigarettes from Eileen. The latter

gazed at her in wonderment, testing how far she would go. The old woman began to wear three coats all at the one time. She tried to go to the bathroom as little as possible: she was hoarding her pee.

'The old woman will live forever,' Eileen screamed. 'She will never die. She will take me with her to the grave. She will hoard me. She will tie string round me, and take me with her to the grave. And the innocent selfish ferns will spring from me. And the baby will feed head down in it, its legs working.'

'No,' she said to Harry, 'I don't want to.'
   'Why not? What's wrong with you?'
   'I don't want to. It's like the bee.'
   'What bee?'
   'The bee, I tell you.'
   'For Christ's sake,' he said. The bee sucked at her body. It sucked her breasts in a huge wandering fragrance.

'I don't know you,' said her mother. 'Who are you? Are you the insurance lady? I'm not giving you any more money. You're after all my money. Are you the coalman? Eileen should pay for that. She owes me ten thousand pounds. I saw that in the paper.'
   'It will cost ten thousands pounds,' Eileen said to Harry.
   'What will?'
   'The baby. To bring it up. It was in the paper. I don't want to have it. It will want its own snooker table. It will smile and smile and be a villain.'

'You will have to go,' Harry told Terry.
   'What for?'
   'Because I can't do anything with you.'
   'What do you mean? You'll be sorry.'
   'Are you threatening me?'
   'No, I'm not threatening you. But you'll be sorry. You'll wake up one day and say to yourself: Did I destroy that boy?' And Terry began to cry.

'You won't get anything out of me that way,' said Harry. 'I can see through your tricks. You will have to go.'

'All right. But you'll be sorry. You'll hate yourself.'

'I failed but he went,' said Harry to Eileen. 'And he started to cry before he went. Oh he's so cunning. But there comes a time.'

'A time?'

'Yes, a time to save oneself. It's a duty. I see that now. She will have to go.'

'She?'

'Yes. She'll have to go. There comes a time. I made a mistake. I shall have to act.'

'Act?'

'That's it. Act. She will simply have to go. We can't afford her.'

'What do you mean?'

'What I say. You've done enough. This is not asked of us. I can see that now. Tell her she will have to go.'

'You tell her.'

'Right. I'll tell her.'

The two of them were alone. The house seemed to close in on them.

'What's that?' she said.

'What?'

'The 'phone,' she said.

'It isn't the 'phone. You're imagining things. The 'phone isn't ringing.'

'Yes, it is.'

'No, it isn't.'

The ferns shut off the light. The floor was a huge beach of sand. She saw the child crossing it towards her. It smiled.

'I love you,' she said.

'I love you,' she repeated.

'The Club is quieter now,' he said. 'Ever since he left. We know where we are. I'm putting on weight.'

'Yes, I see that.'

'It's much quieter. He kept us on our toes. Everyone is obedient.'

'Yes.'

The child cried.

'I love you,' she said. The circle closed again. The baby smiled and smiled and laughed and laughed. It wobbled on unsteady legs among the ferns.

'I'm wounded,' she said, 'between the legs. Between the legs.' And its hairy head blossomed there. 'Between the legs. I'm wounded,' she said.

In the operating theatre on the snooker table its wild cry came towards her.

She cradled the globe of its wet head, which had streamed out of the earth.

Her hands closed, opened.

'I love you,' she said, 'There's nothing else for it.'

The 'phone rang. There was heavy breathing. 'You'll be sorry,' said a voice.

'He never gives up,' said Harry. 'But I don't care.'

'He has become remorseless,' she thought. 'We have been infected.' And she clutched the baby's head to her breast. 'We inherit the disease,' she thought.

The baby warbled in its own kingdom. 'Isn't he beautiful?' she said.

'Yes.'

And the baby burbled like an unintelligible 'phone.

A TRAVELLER'S ROOM

Elspeth Davie

Every other summer I and my young brother with my father and mother came up from the south to visit my aunt and grandmother in the far north of Scotland. On the way, as part of the holiday, we used to stay over one or two nights, and always at a different place.

The time I am particularly remembering we stayed at Perth, having been given the name of a woman who let rooms in that town. We arrived late. The house was within sound of the river. There must have been heavy rains in the previous week or so for it was in full spate – so turbulent that when our landlady Mrs Crawford threw open the door we hardly heard a word she said – only her lips moving rather irritably, her eyes blinking in the first lights of the street. When we were in and the door closed, she finished what she'd been saying. We were reminded that she had not known the exact time of our arrival nor whether we would be wanting supper. Reassuring her that we'd had some food on the way, we asked about our rooms. There were two bedrooms downstairs, she said – one at the back for my father and mother. My brother could have the small room at the front. I remember how I envied him at first. He would be able to escape, unseen and quickly in the early morning, with time to explore the unfamiliar streets before breakfast.

Then I heard our landlady remark, 'I have given your daughter the traveller's room. He has gone further this time. He will not be back for another day or two.' I could see at once of course how jealous my brother was of these words – 'the traveller's room'. This was the sort of thing that, young as he was – and he was younger indeed than myself – he would claim should be given to him, absolutely and automatically, as a

69

man's right. He stood with his hand on the banister, staring up with shining, angry eyes, contending the luck and the justice of my being on the stair at all. I followed Mrs Crawford to the landing above. I climbed very slowly, proudly, like those mountaineers who have been taught to plod carefully, steadily, step by step, no matter how eager to reach the goal. I felt instinctively that it was my right to have a traveller's room since already I had all the longings and restlessness of such a person myself. It was only fair and fitting that the honour of the place should fall to me, even though I was a girl.

I waited with Mrs Crawford at the door of the room. She opened it cautiously as though its privacy must never be disturbed whether he was in Greenland or Timbuctoo. I was disappointed at first sight of the place – a small, rather stuffy room with its bleak flat bed and a grey sofa at the foot of it. There was a rug on the sofa – a knitted rug with a sewn-on border of knitted red birds and blue flowers. My heart sank for a moment. It was unlike him. Still, every man might have someone who sat and knitted for him, misguidedly, night after night. It was not necessarily his fault. There were no books and no pictures in the room and no mementos of other places. Yes, I was disappointed at first, but then at that age one starts digging at once and deeply for hidden treasure. For it must be there. Why, otherwise would one be there oneself unless to discover it under its usual disguise – the grey, commonplace blanket that is deliberately, mufflingly drawn up over every thing and person the moment they are off guard. I knew this myself for my grandfather had suffered this extinction. He had been a fierce and handsome man, hard as a Viking, tough as the figurehead of a ship. The moment he died he was turned into a kindly old fellow. His endearing and eccentric ways were spoken about in the family. In other words, the woolly, grey blanket had covered him up from head to foot.

Almost as if she'd picked up my thought Mrs Crawford said, 'I think you will be comfortable enough here. I have made up that bed of course, but if you do need more blankets you'll find them in the cupboard on the landing.' As soon as she'd left the room I opened the window and as I did so caught sight of a small bird in a cage swinging above me. This was so alarmingly unlooked-for in a man who could have his pick of flamingoes, parrots and even the albatross of the polar seas that I went at once to the door and called down to her, 'Look, do I have to have the bird here? He doesn't want it in his room and neither do I!' She looked up, gave me a peculiarly sharp look, and said, 'That *is* his bird. He's devoted to it. Please don't move anything at all, will you? And put that back at once.' I hooked it up again. The bird hopped to its perch where it swung, its beady eyes watching me in scorn.

I sat down on the bed. At that age I didn't particularly wish to be comfortable, nor perhaps to be happy either. It was excitement I was looking for. New places and new happenings. Downstairs my mother was calling me. There was a blue fog round the bottom stair with the frying fumes of chips. Mrs Crawford was scooping crisp bits of haddock onto plates. My brother started to eat quickly, still full of restless jealousy, wondering what strange portents and discoveries I had come upon in the room above. His own room, he said, was nothing more than a storeroom. He was to sleep with brooms, old water-proofs, wilting pot-plants and an ancient sewing-machine which would cruelly bar the way if he had to get up quickly in the night.

'Are you comfortable up there yourself?' my father asked quickly.

'Well, not exactly comfortable,' I replied mysteriously, my eyes still on my brother. 'The room's too strange for that. And I daresay I'll have strange dreams. He must be an odd person. I don't think he's like us at all. He doesn't need the sort of things we do, of course. He's never stayed long enough in one place to want them, you see.'

'Things?' my father repeated. 'Such as?'

'Well – cushions,' I said vaguely. 'Pictures, mats, good soap, mirrors – all that sort of thing.'

'Well then, I daresay you're right,' said my father brusquely. 'If he doesn't care for cushions and even soap he's certainly not like us.'

71

'Does that mean you haven't got a pillow on your bed?' my mother asked anxiously, innocent of the insult to Mrs Crawford, who immediately flushed. 'She has *two* pillows,' she exclaimed, 'and a bolster in the cupboard if she really must have one.' When we had apologized she came out of the kitchen holding a bowl and, putting two thumbs on the bottom of it, shook out a fine, brown steamed pudding, high as a hat, onto a plate.

I was too tired that night to look at my room again. I slept deeply and woke to the sound of wheels grinding past, the honking of horns and a great commotion of voices under my window. It was the time of the large exodus of the pickers from Perth out to the raspberry fields some miles away. I looked out. Whole families filled the lorries – men, women and children, grandparents and small babies, piled around with their belongings. Carts, trucks, bicycles and tractors accompanied them. Big dogs span, howling, from the bicycle wheels. Even the odd cat had crept up to sleep amongst the bundles at the back of the lorries. The work was ill-paid, often long, cold and wet, but there was a feeling of festivity, even adventure, in the air. Most of the pickers camped down around the fields, or in the huts provided, for the whole season, but a few might come back to Perth at sunset, their fingers stained bright red in the fading light, big, crimson blotches on the front of their overalls. They were travellers too, but that first morning I couldn't see it.

After breakfast my brother and I went out to explore the town, crossed the bridge and walked along the river where the water was calmer now. We seldom talked together but now, with two days in an unfamiliar place and a second journey ahead, we broke through the dumbness that overtook us at home. I told my brother that the second part of the journey would be even better than the first because we were still going north. I reminded him that going further and further north was always better – more mysterious, more difficult, but better. Often in summer, I said, you might see the shifting curtains of coloured light and have a hint of polar regions. And in winter the afternoon sky was a peculiar blue-green colour, never seen in the south. At midnight the sky was blacker, the stars brighter. It was lonelier in the north – bare, rocky and wind-swept. Those who travelled to the far north came back with different songs and stories – colder, blacker and more bitter. This was where we were going. Did he understand? Was he ready for it again? No, my brother said. Being younger, he hated to agree with me. No, no, he said, the south was better, and the further south the better it got. Of course the south was better. The downs where we lived were better. He liked the soft chalk and the hard flint. He liked the eye-blinding cliffs. The villages of the south were much, much better. 'Oh of course, if you're talking about *prettiness*!' I exclaimed scornfully, hoping to shame him into admission that no male should ever use the word. 'That's exactly what I *am* talking about,' he replied. He was a creature of extremes. Going south, he didn't stop at the cliffs. Not bothering what I thought, he went lightly through orchards and flowering meadows, on and on through heat as far as deserts – until he came to the camels with trails of blue-cupped footprints in the sand. I knew it was nothing but the poster he'd seen in a travel agents. But he had now advanced into tropical forests. By this time he seemed much younger than me, as though he'd unwittingly stepped back into fairy tale. Still, there was no end to the north–south argument. We had to finish by agreeing that you came to snow and ice at either end if you went far enough. Finally my brother said he hoped we wouldn't have to go every single year of our lives to the north. He kept his most outrageous saying to the end, however – till we were back again near the safety of the house. 'And I don't *like* my grandmother! Don't *like* my aunts either!' I, who had always been a rather conventional child, never doubting the value of family relationships, was deeply disturbed by this outburst.

During the afternoon it started to rain – a continuous, misty rain that went on for the rest of the day. I spent most of it reading upstairs. After a time I put the book down and looked about me at the traveller's room. I felt there must be something I had missed. Even in the rooms of ordinary people there was more to discover. Behind the bed there was a narrow shelf with a curtain which I pulled aside. It revealed a pair of pink bedroom slippers. They were not exactly fur-lined but they were soft, worn and kneaded into the shape of knobbled toes. I felt the premonition of some sadness in another person – not a sharp, penetrating sadness, but the slow, enveloping kind that folds in forever to keep out air and light. Such a sadness in myself or anyone else was the last thing I wanted to feel. This was for older persons – a matter of dark nights and grey awakenings – coming on slowly like rheumatism and with no fuss or drama about it. It would be simply, vaguely grey. It would be like being lost in a mist. Further back on the shelf I had missed a pair of shoes. Certainly these were stronger, meant for walking, and in that way had more hope about them. But the toes were scuffed, the laces thin, and when I turned them over I saw the heels worn down in a defeated curve. I put my feet into the slippers for a moment and took a few steps in them. Certainly they were huge and comfortable, but sad like a great sigh of relief. I was thankful to take them off.

Supper on that second night was more silent. Towards the end of it my parents discussed whether they would go out to look in on an acquaintance they had known years ago in the place. We were left with Mrs Crawford who told us how hard her life had been since her husband died. She showed us the yellowing photos, the tangled fishing-tackle and even the half bottle of whisky he had left. He'd been a builder and had worked on most of the newer houses in the town. She asked me what I meant to be when I grew up. 'I'm going to be a gym teacher,' I said. 'But also of course a traveller like the man upstairs.'

'No woman can be that,' she remarked with some triumph. Several times she said what women could or couldn't be.

'Well, what did *you* want to be?' I asked. 'I mean before you were married.'

'I was a nurse,' she replied. I was astonished. It was difficult to imagine her walking about between beds, spooning out medicines and propping up patients. 'I met my husband in a hospital bed,' she remarked not without dignity. 'And of course that sort of training's never lost. It even comes in useful if a lodger should fall ill.'

'Well, surely your present man can't often fall ill,' I said, uneasy at the thought.

'Oh, but very often in winter. He has a chest, you see. But it's not to be wondered at, is it? He's very undemanding, though – quiet and retiring, so I'm not complaining.' For a moment I stood, thinking unhappily of a retiring, uncomplaining, flat-out traveller who had a chest but not the right sort – not one containing loot, but a quietly wheezy one. We stood together silently for a time. I wondered what could make her extra work worthwhile. She looked a person not to be put upon for long.

'He must come back with interesting stories,' I suggested. 'The places and the people.' As a matter of fact I wondered whether she might actually love the man. At school we'd done a lightning-quick run through Shakespeare. I happened to know Desdemona had fallen for Othello on account of his travellers's tales.

'Places and people!' Mrs Crawford looked scornful. 'Well, I've lived here all my life. I think I know as much about these parts as I want to know.'

We left it at that, and soon I retreated again to my room. I had put almost nothing in the wardrobe but I opened it all the same. To make room for me Mrs Crawford had squashed all his things to one side. I looked at them. They made a thin bunch, pressed together in their dark corner as if hiding. There was nothing husky here, nothing exotic either and nothing for blazing heat or fierce cold. There was a rather shabby overcoat with a torn pocket and one very smart suit, very carefully pressed, its shoulders covered with a hood of newspaper. I hung up my own coat thoughtfully. Even this schoolgirl's raincoat looked more confident than his things. In the narrow drawer of one compartment there were two pairs of gloves. The difference between these pairs surprised me. One pair looked almost new, carefully wrapped in tissue paper. The other was what my mother would call the 'wearing pair' which meant they were for every day and probably rather miserable days at that. They made me feel for the first time how vulnerable and expressive hands were – sometimes confident and commanding, sometimes exhausted and hopeless. This wearing pair was certainly hopeless, as if there were no bones at all in the owner's fingers, as though anything he might pick up would fall helplessly from his hands. In a flash all notion of him finding a route up some unknown mountain faded. Gloves or no gloves, there was no way he could put these tired fingers into the icy fissures between rocks. At the same time all thought of the travelling star disappeared – that one who takes a leap at a passing train and grips the handrail even as his pursuer grips his ankle. I picked the gloves up and let them dangle from my hand. The fingers were fat, curved and powerless as sausages. The other gloves were remarkable in a different way. Too spruce, too tight to be anything but for show. I put my hands into the poor, loose gloves and thought about this man. It was not true to say I was disappointed in this traveller. No, I was disappointed in myself for not understanding him better.

When I heard my parents come in I went downstairs. They were depressed, having discovered that one partner of the couple they'd gone to visit had died the year before. 'How awful that we shouldn't have known,' said my mother.

'But who was there here to let us know?' my father replied.

The idea of death was now beginning to pervade the house upstairs and downstairs. No doubt from what Mrs Crawford had said even the man above could die before he'd properly explored the globe. To die before your best leather gloves wear out! Worse still, to die of some tear or split inside your body before even your torn and shabbiest gloves wear out!

'I didn't know them,' said Mrs Crawford, 'or I would certainly have let you know. I didn't even see the death in the paper.'

'How would you see the death without knowing the name?' said my brother. 'Don't names and deaths go together in the paper?' My brother was told to be quiet and show some respect for the dead and for Mrs Crawford.

So it went on circling in my head for the rest of the evening –

death and names, death and respect, death and gloves, death and chests, empty wardrobes and heavy coffins. It was now dark – time to go to bed. I went up slowly by myself. They had filled even the hall and the stairs with death. I wondered whether the stairs were too steep for the traveller with his poor chest. One night Mrs Crawford would hear a thud on the top step and that would be the end of travel. The door below me opened suddenly. 'Miss Foster, would you be careful to keep the room tidy up there. Mr Pennycuick should be coming back tomorrow afternoon and I'd like him to find everything just as he left it.' Probably she was the first person who'd ever called me by my full name and I was very grateful for it. I told her I would be extremely careful of the room and that every item of my own would be removed long before he returned. 'Don't think I want to turn you out,' she went on, 'but I know you'll be moving on tomorrow afternoon. And he *is* rather particular – that's to say, tidy. I suppose he has to be in his way of life. It wouldn't do for him to appear careless.' I myself had hoped that Mr Pennycuick's main attribute was to be supremely carefree – far more so than the rest of us. And surely the carefree had more than a dash of carelessness in their make-up?

I closed the door behind me and began mechanically tidying the place. There was little to put away for there was so little there. I took out my coat and crushed his frail clothes more closely together at the end of the wardrobe. I didn't look at the top shelf there. I think now I was afraid of finding a hat – just possibly a bowler or even what was called a golfing hat. Frequently on our walks at home I had been warned to stand absolutely still and dead silent while a group of men, quaintly dressed, walked slowly across to pick up white balls on a stretch of sacred green. Occasionally someone walked behind pushing a bag on wheels. I pushed the soft slippers further into the shelf and as I did so a little book fell on the floor. I picked it up with all the eagerness one gives to the discovery of a stranger's life – his interests, opinions and prejudices, his friends and enemies, what he says and what he reads. This book was a piece of the pattern I needed, so to speak. I didn't intend sleeping for a long time yet. If need be, and if it wasn't too complicated a work, I would read the whole book. I began turning the pages. This was a good-natured book, you could call it a compassionate one. It was a book of recipes – not the day-to-day sort, but ones lovingly concocted and written up for those who had to be a little careful of their digestion. I read further. They were good, kindly recipes – no Eastern spices or harsh curries there. They were milky, beige and bland, none of them highly-flavoured. There were a few coloured photos of course, of pale cakes, pale sauces and custards and a few special fruits. It was not invalid food, but food for delicate, domestic stomachs. Yet I was comforted, remembering that even armies were said to travel on their stomachs, and armies included wayfarers of every kind – tramps, travellers, daredevils and adventurers. I imagined Mr Pennycuick, a weary Ulysses, lying down at last after long journeys, having escaped the spicy isles, drifted past seductive gardens of exotic fruit, circumnavigated the seas of poisonous fish and firmly trodden the great iced mountains of white sugar. Yes, he would be weary, but he had come through. Even if he died in the night he would die a hero.

I woke to a sunny morning, dressed quickly and went to the window where below me I saw another procession of berry pickers heading for the fields. Again the bicycles, carts, tractors and lorries went by loaded with people. And again I could not see them as travellers. They were going only a few miles and to the familiar fields they had returned to year after year. Yet they showed the same boisterous freedom of people going to the ends of the earth. One man waved a broad, black hat to me as he passed on his high lorry. A woman raised her kettle out of a basket towards me in a friendly, mocking gesture. They were soon out of sight and the rumble of cartwheels, the hooting lorries, bicycle bells and barking dogs faded away into the distance.

I took one last look round the room before I left it, intent on removing every scrap of myself before Mr Pennycuick took over. However far he'd gone, he'd left this room in good faith, believing that nothing would be disturbed. I was the usurper, the spy and the interloper. I knelt to pick a thread from my jumper off the mat, smoothed a wrinkle in the coverlet, shut the window and closed the door behind me for the last time.

All morning I waited downstairs for the traveller to return. My father and mother were quietly packing up their stuff and we were to have lunch in town before an afternoon train. Mrs Crawford was in the kitchen preparing a late meal for her lodger. It was very different from our first morning. Nothing was for us now. Our landlady was not interested. The house was geared to its true occupant. And it seemed as though the whole house had widened out to receive him, to receive this wanderer, huge with the happenings of the last days, the last weeks and months. As time drew on I cast all doubts from my mind. This man, without looking down, would see us all – even my father – as though from some height. Whatever his actual size he would appear tall, for tallness was associated with an all-round view of the world, measured against the straight line of a distant horizon on land and sea. A tall man, then, with long, striding legs and long arms for hauling himself up out of danger.

It must have been after two o'clock when I heard a key in the front door. I had been doing my hair before the mirror in the hall. I turned quickly, combing my hair behind my ears with my fingernails to allow me to hear the sound more clearly. For though the key still scratched at the lock it was rather a timid sound, as of a man very quietly letting himself into a house not his own.

'Well, hullo there!' he said, coming in and shutting the door softly behind him. He was very short and stocky, neat and dapper in an out-of-date way. His suit was dark grey with a soft matching hat worn at a slant in an attempt to look daring and hopeful, but which in fact covered half his right eye in a despondent tilt. He carried a large suitcase, very well polished in patches but worn at the corners. The handle seemed thin and shiny with the sweat of years.

Through the half-open door leading from the passage we saw Mrs Crawford irritably stabbing at a fish in a pan. 'I'm sorry to be so late,' he said. 'I see you've all been waiting for me.'

'Oh no, not at all,' I replied with pitiless politeness. '*They* may have been expecting you. I was expecting someone else.' He thought about this for a moment, staring over my head in an abstracted way. 'No doubt, no doubt,' he murmured at last. 'All the same, here I am. This is where I live. With any luck I shall keep my room for a long time yet.' I began to be rather afraid of this man and his insistence on who he was and where he should be. It was not a fear of the man himself, but of those totally unexpected reversals in life – how all adventures can be flattened at one blow, how heroes are simply tired men, how I myself was only a stupid child and not at all the clever girl I had imagined. Our new arrival was now shaking hands with my parents in the sitting room. He then moved out into the kitchen and I followed him. 'Well, how did it go this time?' asked Mrs Crawford.

'Not well at all,' said the man. 'I don't know why, but no, not well.'

'It's not the best time of year,' she said. 'Too many folk away.'

'No, I don't think that was it,' he said. 'I mostly managed to get them in all right, but with very little luck.'

'Well, let me see,' said Mrs Crawford. Obediently he knelt on the linoleum. I saw a pair of shoes, twins to the ones upstairs – narrow and hurtfully smart with the rubber worn down at the heels. He opened up his case and took out the brushes, the dusters, the cleaning fluids, the scouring stuffs, the polishes, the perfumed lavatory liquids, and lined them up, one by one. Finally he took out a handful of red, yellow and green toothbrushes.

'Take one,' he said, handing them to me.

'No, really – it's all right,' I said.

'Take one, take it before you go. You *are* going, aren't you?' he gently added. Indeed he sounded thankful that I was going. I knew what he meant. I had stood around with my sad face long enough, watching him gather his own disappointment together. Mrs Crawford had been watching my face as I stared at the brushes and dusters. 'Don't worry,' she said, 'one day, before you know where you are, you'll be using every one of those, and very thankful for them too!'

We left about fifteen minutes later. The river was full again, as when we arrived. I looked up at the small, sealed bedroom window above, and below it at the two figures framed in the doorway. They were waving. Neither my brother nor I waved back. We had said our goodbyes. As for myself, I wanted to forget all that was fixed and shut and framed about the house. I wanted to forget the wardrobe, the birdcage, the suitcase and the groggy chest. I kept my eyes fixed with inhuman calm upon the water flowing on its reckless voyage from the mountain to the river, and – moving with a greater river further out – swiftly, finally to the open sea.

MAGICIAN

Richard Dingwall

Manipulating the Symbols

Remember me standing on a chair on the landing with that doll in my hand hanging over the railing, hair dangling, you crying, Gwen shouting?

Susie's eyes are blue, her hair is brown like her mother's used to be. She is screaming: My dolly! Mine! Benny says, It's all right. I just want to try something. He is standing on the chair, doll in hand. He is holding it by the foot. A second floor flat.

Remember the green banister paint? Stair green Jacko called it, as if all the banisters in Edinburgh were painted the same colour and always had been. And the steps, brown stone worn hollow. Time.

It's all right, Susie, he says, I just want to try something.

Illusion

Remember Jacko standing in the kitchen with a false moustache and a pack of cards? He shuffles, he cuts one-handed, he riffles, he does a spread and turnover.

A normal pack you'll see.

Gwen was a modern mother, she always let us use her first name, hated to be called Mum.

She is laughing. Jacko bows, presents the pack.

Take a card, any card.

Me? she says. More laughter. No!

Take a card. And she reaches. Not that one! says Jacko teasing and pulls the pack away but slowly so that her hand follows.

Gwen stretching. Susie screaming. Me! Me! Let me! Benny

pushes her. Shut up stupid. Gwen laughing, her hand straying after the pack that Jacko holds.

And . . .

Her hand straying after the pack that Jacko holds.

Not that one, he says.

She takes the card, a King of hearts. Let me see, says Benny. Me! Me! King of hearts back in the pack. Gwen cuts, Jacko shuffles, cuts, fumbles. The card is in Susie's ear. Shuffles, cuts, shuffles. It is in Benny's pocket. Shuffles, cuts. Gwen is crying.

Jacko and Gwen necking on the couch. Gwen in the green dress she wears dancing. The tops of her nylons are showing.

Leave 'em Laughing

Benny and Susie in a club somewhere in Yorkshire. A corner table. He drinks gin and lime, she martini with an olive.

Did you see the act? she says. The hall is brown, cavernous. On the stage a teenage pop group are playing badly.

It's getting better, says Benny.

Better, she says. Shit! Remember . . . she says but he interrupts her.

Remember the doll, he says.

Candy.

What?

The doll's name was Candy.

I thought it was called Lulu, he says.

No. That was the one with red hair.

Remember me standing on the chair, blonde-haired Candy in my hand, two flights up, dangling her over the stairwell, you looking on, crying?

That was after Jacko.

Yes, after Jacko. Gwen was into mini-skirts then. Remember?

Benny! Gwen at the door. The doll's hair dangling, stiff as if bleached too often.

I just want to try something.

83

Benny lets go, the doll falls. Benny smiles, master of the provocative moment. Susie screaming. Gwen shouting, You little bastard, I'll . . . The doll falls, pauses in mid-air then leaps back into Benny's hand. Tarrah!

Green elastic.

Appearances are Important

Jacko, a wiry man with a Billy Fury hair style (*Halfway to Paradise*). Good teeth (a ready smile, winning), a charmer. Later (after Gwen, they saw him round the clubs) he affected tinted glasses, had a perm. Jacko with curly brown hair, chewing gum. Proud of his body, 29-inch waist. Jacko, two hands on his backside, looking over his shoulder . . . 'a bum of distinction'.

Gwen: blonde (naturally brunette) follower of fashion (see above). Red cheeks, heavy breasts, thick thighs. Likes to laugh, likes to dance. Two children.

Preparation

There was one trick that required a lot of newspaper to be torn into small pieces.

Gwen irritated. Jacko, come on!

Susie on the couch, crying.

Gwen: Benny! Stop that!

What? Innocence.

You know fine what I'm talking about. Susie, belt up will you. Jacko! For Christ's sake!

Okay, Okay.

(Smell of burning from the stove.)

Jacko!

Never Do the Same Trick Twice for the Same Audience

He was good to her, says Susie.

Benny shrugs. A roar from the crowd. A striptease number finishes.

Ever think of going in for that caper? He nods at the

bare-breasted woman clumping down from the stage in her stiletto heels.

Wrong shape, pal, she says. I'm like mum. Dumpy.

Jacko liked them that way.

Terrific. A one man fan club. Anyway he never paid to look.

Remember . . . says Benny. Susie interrupts. Remember me standing at the top of those stairs shouting, Stop! Stop! Gwen at the door, swearing?

I just want to try something, says Benny. I want to see what happens. And drops the doll. Falling doll. Doll fall. Green elastic. Magic.

Susie crying. Gwen slaps his ear.

Stupid bloody trick!

Benny indignant: It's my magic.

Stupid. Bloody.

It's easy. Look.

Green elastic. Fingers slip . . .

Distraction

Saturday night. Gwen and Jacko watching telly. Gwen curled up, head on Jacko's lap. Jacko's arm along the back of the couch, hand on Gwen's breast, beer bottle by his feet. Lights off. Eyes reflect grey light. Kids in bed.

The door opens. Susie crawls across the floor, takes the beer bottle back to the door. (Jacko watching telly.) To the door where Benny waits. He drinks a mouthful of beer then hands the bottle to Susie who pretends to sip, makes a face. Benny replaces the swallowed beer by pissing in the bottle. Susie crawls across the floor, puts the bottle back.

Saturday night. Gwen and Jacko watching telly on the couch. Jacko drinking beer. Secret laughter from the hall.

Bloody kids!

Sleight of Hand

Remember Jacko in top hat and opera cloak. Tails. The lot. Tossing coins, finger palming. (The transmutation of base metals into . . . well, half crowns.)

See this washer? The original brass razzoo. (A disbelieving
audience giggles.) It's the truth! Got it off an Abyssinian sailor
in The Double-Headed Crown. (The mention here of the
Abyssinian, an unlikely exotic, and the weak joke on the name
of the local pub, The Crown, damage his credibility.)

Jacko tosses the washer with the right hand and catches it
with the left which he then shows us empty. The washer is in the
right.

It's the truth, he says, now looking through the hole in the
washer at his small audience. Susie and Gwen, the credulous
ones, the mugs, are on the couch oohing and aahing, brown
head and blonde head leaning together giggling. Benny on the
floor, looking up, watching the other hand, the one that's not
moving.

Benny says later: He was good. Technically he was brilliant
but he had no sense of . . .

Flair, says Susie.

I don't know, says Benny. I mean he had the top hat, the
cloak, a sort of showmanship, you know?

Jacko and Gwen arguing.

There was a ten bob note in my purse.

Jacko raises his hands, a ready smile. Search me, he says. Fat
lot of good that would do me!

Susie at the door watching. Benny in the bedroom sucking
fruit gums, fingering 9/6d change.

A brass razzoo. Jacko tosses the coin again, an arc. It hangs
too long and changes colour in mid-air. He catches it in his left
hand. A gold doubloon! He pulls a silk scarf from nowhere.

He made it look too easy, says Benny.

Cutting the Lady in Half

She hits the bottom stair landing on her head. Even two flights
up they hear the crack. The blonde head lies still, one blue eye
staring up. A depressed fracture of the skull.

Susie crying. Gwen shouting. Benny smiles reassuringly. He
puts his finger on the soft patch under the hair. It crumbles

leaving a triangular hole. Fragments of bakelite rattle in the hollow skull. Later he will prise out the eyes to see how they work but now he smiles again. It's all right, he says.

Remember . . . he starts to speak again but Susie interrupts him. Jacko was important, she says.

Who for? This from Benny.

The band is back, playing very loud. They won't get booked again. Susie is speaking but Benny misses most of what she says. She mentions Gwen's name several times.

The door is closed. Gwen crying. Susie whining. Closed door. Door.

Where's Jacko gone? This is Susie, Gwen doesn't say anything. Want Jacko!

Closed door having slammed. Door.

Benny watches to see if he will come back. Through the window perhaps or down the chimney. Another trick, you know?

He was the one, says Susie shouting over the band.

Billy, the club secretary is standing at the side of the stage signalling the band to finish their set and come off. The singer is looking the other way, the guitarist mimes dumb ecstasy to sustain and feed back on his top A.

She never was the same afterwards, says Susie.

She's all right, says Benny holding up doll Candy for them to see. Let's play at hospitals, Susie. See, Candy needs a bandage on her sore knee. See if we can make it better.

And For My Next Trick
The band are off now. Billy pulled the plug leaving them idiot dancing with empty instruments on an unlit stage, the pounding drummer stranded. For a while it looked like they wouldn't leave but they saw various members of the committee gathering in the wings. The patrons shouted words of encouragement.

Stay where you are, son. Let him kick your head in. That sort of thing.

I used to think of him as my father, Susie says. I used to pretend.

Benny shakes his head. No, he says.

I went into their room, Gwen's room I mean, she says, and looked through all the drawers. This was after he'd gone. I looked in all the cupboards. I thought he was magic, really magic.

Benny sips green lime and gin. Have you met her latest man? he asks. Susie wrinkles her nose.

You'll be on soon, she says.

After Billy does his stuff.

The secretary is telling jokes while they clear the stage.

I looked in all the drawers, says Susie. I found a pack of cards. They were all Kings of hearts.

Not a magician, says Benny. Just another conjuror.

Billy has started the spiel. They hear Benny's name mentioned and glance expectantly at the stage. The spotlight finds their table. Benny stands and toasts them with his drink. He passes a hand in front of the glass and the contents have changed from green to red. Applause. Billy calls his name. The house band plays 'That Old Black Magic'.

THE BAGPIPING
PEOPLE

Douglas Dunn

Two or three mornings a week, in summer, a tinker called Robertson bagpiped the Gilchrist family from sleep half an hour before the time set on its alarm clocks. He played on the hoof, walking along the edge of a narrow plantation of birch trees.

'I thought you liked bagpipes,' said Jim Gilchrist, teasing his father's short temper at the breakfast table. 'Any time there's a pipe band on the wireless, you always have it turned up. You're the man who wants to go to the Edinburgh Tattoo. Military nostalgia,' he said, with a lighthearted, sneering conclusiveness. 'It's like a plague in this country. I don't suppose you noticed, but last winter there seemed more pipe bands on the wireless than usual. Suez.'

'Is that a fact?' Mr Gilchrist replied.

'No different,' said Jim, 'from these countries you read about where the radio stations pump out military music while the rebels and the government troops fight it out on the streets. Hungary,' he said, the way he had said 'Suez' a moment before.

'I worry about your mind,' said his father, before tasting his first spoonful of porridge. 'Aw, Sadie! You haven't salted it! Again,' he said wearily, plopping his spoon into his plate.

'I did salt it,' his wife said, with her back to them as she turned the frying bacon and eggs with a fish server. Almost to herself, she added, 'I salted it the same as I always salt it.'

Sam Gilchrist's porridge never seemed salty enough on these mornings when Robertson's piping woke him up at six. While he sprinkled extra salt on his porridge, his son measured a spoonful of sugar and then, when he knew his father was watching him, sifted it over his porridge.

'Men,' Mr Gilchrist said, with a jab of his spoon, 'don't put sugar on their porridge.'

'I don't see why not,' Jim said. 'You put jam on your cheese.'

'When the tinker's pipes make him so bad-tempered,' Mrs Gilchrist said, 'you'd think he'd take the trouble to ask the man to play half an hour later, when he's up anyway. Would that be unreasonable?'

'Perfectly reasonable,' said Jim.

His father left the table and opened both kitchen windows. Robertson's piping was too far away to be loud, but there was no doubting it was there.

'They're tinkers,' said Sadie Gilchrist. 'They're used to taking a telling. Used to it,' she emphasized, 'week in, week out. It's not as if your father would be asking him never to play within our hearing. Half an hour. What's half an hour in a busy day?'

'I don't mind when or where he plays,' said Gilchrist.

'He says he doesn't mind.' She sighed with disbelief. 'You minded, loudly, at six this morning! He says he doesn't mind! You should've heard him.'

The Robertsons and other tinker families lived in an untidy encampment two fields away from the Gilchrists' house. Tarpaulins were stretched over arched metal supports to form tents. It looked like a village of nomadic tribesmen. They possessed a small, open-backed lorry, three horse-drawn carts, and a number of ponies that grazed on lane-side grass or in the waste ground between the pillboxes and blast walls of a wartime anti-aircraft gun position.

By nine in the morning, Robertson would take up his station on the tree-darkened minor road that descended to the ferry. All day in summer, he piped up and down the queues of waiting cars. At times, the queues were long and profitable. Often in bad weather, only a few cars waited in a short, wet line. Commercial vehicles, whose drivers were working and not on the road for pleasure, gave no money and were a waste of the piper's wind and skill. Robertson wore a kilt, brown jacket, and off-white open-necked shirt, and went sockless in a pair of brown brogues blanched by a lack of polish and too much weather and walking. He was followed by his daughter. She was about seventeen, and she wore the same green dress day after day, and the same patched sweater. The only variation in her clothing was a light scarf she tied under her chin. Red-haired, flushed, sullen, and barefooted for effect, she had the job of rattling the change in her cloth moneybag at the windows of each car. When it rained, father and daughter stood together under the overhang of the trees – never in the wooden shelter for pedestrians and cyclists.

To contend with the summer traffic, the ferry employed an extra hand, and for the last three years this summer job had been Jim Gilchrist's. At each end of the dismal vessel was a metal ramp, raised and lowered on chains, which when dropped on the cobbled gradients that led into the water allowed the vehicles to drive on and off. Super-structure on either side of the craft rose to an upper deck with benches that doubled as life rafts. On fine days most passengers went up on deck. In the middle of the ferry there was room for ten cars, fewer if a bus or a lorry or a furniture moving van got there first. Entire cycling clubs, local pedestrians, ramblers, hitchhikers all used the ferry, as well as holidaying motorists, and vans and lorries on every conceivable commercial mission. People came from miles around to watch the ferry's clumsy, clanking, humorous crossings, to wonder at its workhorse appearance, its homely, functional looks, its strength, and then to take a round trip.

Ice cream could be bought from Italian vans on either side of the river. Small boys used the ferry for imaginary adventures. The river stank of oil and an unmistakable, nonspecific industrial aroma compounded of ship-building, engineering, and the city of Glasgow, through which it flowed before reaching there. Often, the ferry waited for freighters to go by. Passengers waved to sailors, and the ships hooted as their wash approached the ferry and waves broke on the cobbled spits, sluicing around the wheels of the cars as they boarded slowly and carefully, and a ferryman ushered them to come on faster.

Ashton, one of the regular conductors, spent much of his time chasing after passengers and asking to see their tickets. He lived in the hope of catching locals from the south bank whom Jim had let on board free of charge. Jim watched Ashton double-checking tickets, and in his turn he kept his eyes open for natives of the north bank whom Ashton's counter-generosity allowed to cross without paying the fare.

'That was my brother you charged, Jim,' Ashton said.

'Sorry, Wattie. I'd no idea.'

'No idea? He crosses this river twice a day! He even looks like me. If you think you can come it wi' me, then forget it. It's no skin off my nose if your father knows a big wheel in the Navigational Trust,' he said, prodding Jim in the chest. 'I'm a lifelong socialist. I don't hold wi' this job-getting through friends of friends or who your daddy knows.'

'So what? I'm a lifelong socialist myself.'

'You? You aren't even weaned yet.'

The ferry was pulled across on parallel chains turned on board in engine houses that were open for small boys and their fathers to watch. 'Lovely piece of engineering!' 'You're doing a fine job there!' men called to the engineer, who felt himself to be the most watched man in Scotland. Each time the vessel left its cobbled, slippery jetties and the tension was taken up on the chains, they whipped out of the water with a dripping shudder. Women hid their faces in their hands with fear that the massive links might snap, and the strange blue-and-white metal box in which they were crossing the river end up drifting at the mercy of the current as helplessly as a biscuit tin.

'Stand back from the chains there!' Ashton's manner had the fulsome pomposity of the ancient trade of ferryman.

'If you had your way, Ashton, you'd ban bridges. Your days are numbered. One day, the twentieth century'll get wise to this contraption.'

When he wasn't playing his pipes and Jim walked past, the tinker always had a civil greeting. 'And how's the wee boatie?'

Like everyone else, Jim brought sandwiches for lunch, but he was the only one who went ashore to eat them. Jim never saw Robertson or his daughter eat anything. They went over the wall beside the ferry ramp, and into the park that surrounded a hospital for disabled and blind ex-servicemen. There they lit a fire in the same spot every day, seven days a week, and brewed tea.

'That's a very old-looking set of pipes you play, Mr Robertson.' Jim imagined that the girl looked surly because she didn't like his knowing their name. It was known among their own kin and kind, but apart from that it was known only to inquisitive policemen, various inspectors from the County Council, and a few farmers. 'How old are they?' Jim asked.

'What would a summer boatie like you know about pipes and pibroch?' said Robertson as he stooped over his fire.

'Nothing,' Jim admitted.

'And you don't look as if you want to learn,' the tinker said slyly, smiling over his tin mug of tea. 'Auld pipes,' he said, 'play auld tunes.'

'I'm one of the few peoples in this world who hear them at six in the morning,' Jim said amiably.

'You've heard me play,' said Robertson, 'you've heard the best you'll ever hear.'

'Would you like a sandwich?' Jim asked father and daughter. 'I've got more than I need. My mother thinks there must be two of me.' The girl nodded a surprised no and walked away, scattering the dregs of her tea on the ground. Strong tea brewed on an open fire and drunk from tin mugs clutched in hot hands is not to be despised, and Jim hoped that Robertson would offer him some. 'I've egg, salmon paste, or dried dates,' he told the tinker.

'No palm trees where I come from,' said Robertson. He took another drink of tea, with an audible slurp.

'I don't suppose my father's complained to you about your six-in-the-morning rehearsals?'

'Your dad and me get on right fine,' said Robertson.

'But you play all day, every day. It must be some strain on the wind. I don't understand why you'd want to play at six in the morning as well.'

'The last time I saw your dad, he was telling me how he fair misses it when I'm gone. He gave me a dozen eggs that time, and he promised to have a word wi' the farmer, Irvine, and pave the way for my two boys, helping them to a paid job for a week or two. Which your father did. He's a man whose word's as good as a deed done. They'll no' find it easy to make that man change as the clock changes, for all his prosperity.'

Summer was Sam Gilchrist's busiest time of the year. He ran a garage, and the major part of his business lay in the sale and repair of tractors and other agricultural machinery. He was beginning to prosper with the nineteen-fifties and saw better times ahead. He worked hard, and it was after seven by the time he got home. He ate, smoked, read the newspaper, dozed with it on his lap; then he woke up and stretched, yawned, and said, 'Right. Bedtime.'

'Your father,' said Sadie Gilchrist, 'is a wonderful conversationalist.'

'I hear you gave the tinker a dozen eggs,' Jim said. 'This is a man who gives handouts to an alarm clock.'

'And you're the man who's over-fond of his bed. Pass them a few eggs now and then,' said Gilchrist, 'and they'll be less inclined to help themselves. I've known men like Robertson go through a hen hut just like that – *psst*,' he said, cutting his throat with his forefinger. 'And there's your eggs gone, and half your hens as well.'

'And then he uses his influence with Sandy Irvine. Jobs,' said Jim, 'for two tinkers. He's even told Robertson how much he dotes on his bagpiping.'

'Don't complain, then,' said Sadie Gilchrist, 'if he serenades us outside the bedroom window.'

'I go a long way back with Robertson. It's not how I'd live, but he has a decent streak, and it suits me to give him a helping hand when I feel like it.'

During his lunch hours, Jim observed the habits of the motorists as Robertson piped and his daughter begged with her jangling moneybag. He saw men and women open their car doors and listen with folklorist attentiveness. In his ferryman's uniform, he felt like a cross between a naval officer and a bus conductor; he noticed them size him up as an object of curiosity. Many people gave the girl a copper coin or two with a smile and good grace. Others wound up their windows and looked away when it came their turn for the tinker's daughter to shake her cloth bag before them. Her look then was sharp and peremptory. Jim saw people begin conversations with their companions when they saw her coming, to give the impression that they were too busy doing something else to notice she was there.

At the busiest times, the queue, the ferry, the riverside had the atmosphere of a fair. Children ran down the line of cars to and from the ice-cream vans. Money changed hands for ice cream, lemonade, and bagpiping. The Hospital for Disabled Ex-Servicemen had a small showroom at its park gate in which the patients displayed and sold their wares in basketwork. Coin boxes for donations towards the hospital's work were carried up and down the queue by volunteers. Hills on the north bank rose high enough to stand as a promise of the Highlands, towards which many of the motorists were headed. At other stopping places – ferries, scenic spots, ruins and castles – they would come across more bagpipers, other conscientious daughters urging them to part with a few pennies. They were like a secret population, these bagpiping people.

'Four years back,' said Ashton, 'there was a piper who took up a pitch on the north shore. He'd no licence for it, so the police moved him on, and thank God for that. There were bagpipes there and bagpipes over there, and in the middle of the very river the two wails met, and the racket made your hair stand on end. No kidding,' he said. 'It made my teeth itch. I hate bagpipes. They remind me of the Army.'

'Somehow,' Jim said, 'I thought you were in the Navy.'

'Funnyman, aren't you?'

'It's the way you talk, Ashton. "Port" this, "starboard" that, "amidships" –'

'I've been watching you, and I've noticed. Don't think there's a lot goes on here that Wattie Ashton doesn't see. I've seen you, sitting on that wall, and I've seen the way you look at that tinker's daughter.' Ashton nodded, approving of his own moral malevolence. 'Call yourself educated?'

Over and back again, over and back again – north bank, south bank, north bank, south bank; with each crossing of the broad river, Jim's hands grew dirtier with the feel of copper coins. Ink and paper from his roll of tickets added to the grime on his fingers, the palms of his hands, creeping up as far as his wrists. Rain clouds massed over Dumbarton Rock, which rose around the bend of the river like a fortified stud on the belt of antique stones round Scotland's waist – Dumbarton, Stirling Castle, Edinburgh Castle. The clouds were dark enough to warn of a summer downpour. It rained that day, and made the work miserable and wet. From the top deck, he saw Robertson and the girl under a tree.

On a Friday evening, having just been paid, Jim took a silver florin from his wage packet and dropped it into the girl's pouch as he passed her. A few seconds later, it bounced off the road in front of him. He saw it roll under a car. He turned round, but she already had her back to him and was shaking her cloth bag at the cars. Robertson noticed, too, but he kept on piping.

'How come,' Jim asked his mother, 'Robertson's daughter would throw back at me the florin I dropped into her bag? I thought we were well in with the tinkers. I mean, free eggs, and my father fixes them up with jobs.'

'For someone who's supposed to have brains,' said Mrs Gilchrist, 'you're not very bright.'

'She threw it back at me,' he said angrily.

'Maybe she likes you,' his mother said. 'If I were a tinker lass whose father set her to begging off other folk, and somebody I liked gave me a coin – more, maybe, than I was used to getting –

then I think I'd throw it back.' She smiled as she watched Jim thinking about what she'd said. 'Don't do anything silly,' she went on. 'It'd be a great waste, you riding the length and breadth on a horse and cart.'

'She's practically a next-door neighbour, and I don't even know her first name. She hasn't said a word to me. It's not like how you think,' he said. 'I'd just been paid, and I felt generous.'

'You so much as kiss her ear,' his mother said, 'and you'll wish you'd been stolen by the fairies. You, me, and your dad would find ourselves at a tinker's wedding – yours. They might look like nothing on earth, but they're very strict when it comes to what might be flitting across your mind.'

Throughout the remainder of the summer, Jim thought about how to speak to the girl. She seemed able to guess whenever he came close to working up the courage. Blank as her expression looked, it was an emptiness that had been brought up on conventions of hostility, and that prepared her for the exercise of that gruff, rude dignity with which she snubbed and avoided him. Every few days, he joined the Robertsons at their fire as they sipped their strong tea. The girl said nothing, and her father did not think it discourteous when she walked away to stand by herself.

'Where did you learn to play?' Jim asked the man.

'My uncle taught me. He was a famous piper. Much better than my father was.' Robertson groaned as he stood up. 'I can huff and puff like the big bad wolf,' he said, 'but it's hard work on the legs.'

At the far end of the clearing, the girl counted the coins in her bag. Robertson doused the fire with what was left of his tea. He picked up his pipes and walked away. Before she followed him, the girl scuffed a foot's worth of leaf mould onto the sizzles of the fire. She didn't even look at Jim. He felt inferior.

'Shy, aren't you?' said Ashton, back at the boat. 'Tongue-tied and bashful. You slow down, she gives you a bad look, and then she gets on wi' her begging. A beggar's what she is, isn't it? Don't you know it? She's as far away from your own kind as a duchess or Lady Mucky-Muck. Will you buy a ticket for a good cause?' He was selling raffle tickets for the Scotland–USSR Friendship Society. 'First prize is a week in Leningrad.'

'What's the second prize?'

'If that's your attitude, then you don't deserve the opportunity of a lifetime which a possible prize-winning ticket would put your way.'

'I suppose Poles and Hungarians get free tickets?'

'Counter-revolutionary trash gets what's coming to it, that's what *it* gets. Forget it,' Ashton said. 'I can see I'm wasting my time.'

On the morning that Robertson's band of tinkers were to leave for their autumn and winter camp, Jim turned up for work an hour early, at half-past six. Ashton was already on board. He scowled at Jim.

'What've I done wrong this time?' Jim asked.

'Nothing.' Ashton gave a shrug of innocence, his mouth opening, his teeth shining, amusement slowly drawing over his face. A late-September breeze nudged at Jim's cap as three tugs in a line went downriver. 'It's your last day, an' I'll be glad to see the back of you. It'll no' be like last year, or the year before. When you cross here in the morning to catch your bus to the university, don't expect any favours when it comes to your fare.'

'I've never heard you laugh, Ashton. When did you last laugh, like a normal person?'

'I laugh when I see a loser. I'm laughing right now.'

There was no sign of Robertson's convoy on the road. Jim said, 'The tinkers are crossing this morning. You listen, Ashton, and you listen good. They're going across, and no fares. If you make an issue of it, you'll wish you hadn't bothered.'

'So that's why you got here before the early-duty car man. Sorry to disappoint you,' Ashton said. He pointed to horse dung on the car deck. One of the piles had been treaded by heavy tyres. 'You being the Tinkers' Friend, I was waiting on you to clean it up. They went through here a good half hour ago.' Ashton dragged on his cigarette, and his smoke trailed in the wind. 'Three horse-drawn vehicles, one lorry, eighteen passengers, six of whom were half-fare, them being underage. You're the man wi' the brain. You can tot that up in a flash, no bother, I'm sure. When did I laugh last? I've been laughing all morning. Here,' he said, handing Jim a shovel. 'Go and clean up what they left you.'

'Are you sure it was them?'

'I've been here since 1933. Would I not recognize them? I looked forward to telling that scabby piper no' to come back, him and his mangy clan. They're like redskins, jumping the reservation. Sure I'm sure. I'd know them a mile away. Why do you think I got here early?'

The wash of a freighter slapped against the ferry and ran over the car deck. Withdrawing waves swept it clean. Jim handed the shovel back to Ashton.

'Where are you going now?' Ashton shouted.

'Up for'ard,' Jim shouted back, 'to wait for your brother. Full fare!'

PARIS

Ronald Frame

Miss Caldwell was the smarter of the pair. At one time customers would tell her she looked like Rosalind Russell. Even in retirement she had kept her figure (with difficulty) and always wore a turban (in the French style) and good accessories and shoes. 'Shoes are a person's give-away,' she liked to say, speaking from her experience as a fashion buyer in one of the last of the great Glasgow stores, which had closed its doors at the tail-end of the 'sixties.

Miss McLeod wasn't so meticulous in her appearance, she chose to think she was more 'discreet'. She used to be a teacher in the prep department of a private boys' school in town and for years she'd worn a sexless black gown over her outfits, so variety hadn't mattered. She hadn't dared to change her ways since then and she dressed now as she'd always done, mutely and respectably, because she never knew when she might spot one of her old pupils in the West End, or be spotted by one of them unbeknown. Somehow she felt she owed it to them, not to seem any different from how they must remember her.

Miss Caldwell and Miss McLeod had met in the late 'sixties, as recently retired ladies and as habituées of Miss Barclay's tea room in Byres Road. Before their introduction they'd each had a partner to have their coffee with, until at about the same time of one never-to-be-forgotten year they'd been abandoned – Miss Caldwell's fellow-buyer (from Wylie and Lochhead) had inexplicably been wooed by an elderly manufacturer of ball-bearings and had married him and gone to live in a nice trim seaside bungalow in Largs; Miss McLeod's friend, who'd been a teacher like her (at the Academy), had returned at sixty-four years old to her calf-country in the windy Mearns – leaving the two Misses, Caldwell and McLeod, seated high-and-dry at adjoining tables and with no one in that roomful of spinsters to speak to.

It was an excellent accident which brought them together, the waitress in starched white linen muddling one's sponge eiffel tower with the other's french fancy. With a gracious wave of her hand and in a throaty voice Miss Caldwell had invited the quietly spoken, bespectacled, beanpole Miss McLeod to join her at her (superior) table in the narrow window wedge of the noisy, high-ceiling'd triangular room. That morning and all the Tuesday and Friday mornings that followed they got on pleasantly enough, just chatting about this and that. It turned out that they hadn't a vast amount in common – Miss Caldwell watched television, Miss McLeod listened to the radio; Miss Caldwell read the *Glasgow Herald*, Miss McLeod the London *Telegraph*. Something else happened to bind them, though. About the third month of the arrangement (they'd learned meanwhile to avoid the topics of television and radio, and referred hardly at all to their different reading) they simultaneously began – consciously, but neither admitting it – to slightly elaborate on what they'd both found they liked to discuss best, themselves.

Miss McLeod 'borrowed' the grandfather of a long-lost friend she'd done her teacher-training with to talk about, a colossal bushy-bearded man who'd been an artist in Paris: that way she felt she could expound with impunity on one of her great interests, Fine Art. Miss Caldwell, who sometimes suspected Miss McLeod dwelled too much on cerebral matters, invented a life which had her working in London in the 1930s, in an up-market store in Regent Street. She hadn't been so lucky, of course, but her stories about 'customers' – Nancy Cunard, Margot Asquith, Lady Mountbatten – sounded quite authentic when she recounted them from gossip she'd picked up from old hands in the Glasgow store's staff rooms.

'Once Marlene Dietrich came in. Did you know she always travelled with thirty-two pieces of luggage? There was a film on television, on 'Saturday Matinée', what was it called? 'Shan-ghai Something' –'

When her memory faltered on a person or a place in her 'past', then Miss McLeod (ever on the look-out through the steamy windows of Miss Barclay's for her boys of years ago) took her cue and struck up again about 'her' grandfather's years of exile from Scotland in *fin-de-siècle* Paris. Every time the city was mentioned Miss Caldwell, resembling one of the manne-quins she talked about in her toning fawns and beiges and velvet turbans, would echo the word, 'Ah, *Paris!*' with her own interpretation of what it meant. When it was her turn to speak again she told Miss McLeod, who found it so hard to concen-trate on such things and remember them, about the hundreds and thousands of French couturiers' wonders smothered in tissue paper she'd unwrapped from bandboxes in the shops that had been her life. To save the situation, Miss McLeod, awk-ward in her heather tweeds and oversized cameo brooches and her stout shoes that had a way of pinching her feet however sensible they looked, recited some more odds and ends of information she'd read about Parisian intellectual life in the 1890s.

'I'd love to go!' exclaimed Miss Caldwell in her pan-loaf front-of-shop vowels. 'Wouldn't you?' Miss McLeod nodded and replied in her more sedate Kelvinside teaching voice, 'Paris in the springtime! It must be a sight worth seeing!' (Both felt rather sorry for having admitted so candidly in the early days of their friendship that, for all the places they claimed they had visited, they'd never been to lovely, immortal Paris on the Seine.)

Paris was often discussed, the word 'holiday' would crop up, yet they resisted being drawn into any of the half dozen travel agents they passed leaving Miss Barclay's after coffee on their two social mornings a week.

They each thought they had their reasons. Miss Caldwell considered that her pension from the store was a little less generous than she might have expected after thirty years of service, and it was hard going keeping herself presentably dressed and stocked up with cosmetics, never mind indulging in foreign adventures. For her part Miss McLeod felt that being seen to be 'careful' with her funds gave her a sort of moral advantage as well as a modicum of mystery, qualities she believed she needed since she so patently lacked her companion's somewhat jaded elegance and style.

By tacit consent Paris remained for them how it had been all along – conveniently in the abstract – and they continued with their stories, retelling them with even more vigour as the months and seasons slipped by. Miss Caldwell talked with glee and much waving of her paste rings about the two elderly sisters who lived on the other side of Atholl Gardens from her, one of whom in middle age had decided on impulse to marry; and after the happy day and the wedding night, had returned the next morning to her sister's flat, suitcases in the taxi, and had never spoken to nor as much as set eyes on her husband in the eighteen years since. Miss McLeod's favourite story sounded more forced and even less likely: she said there was a man of ninety-five living near her in Huntly Gardens, who stayed in his flat alone but set eight places at his dining table for dinner and ate his solitary evening meal with the members of his long-dead family for company; his windows were lit into the night as he played his wind-up gramophone and walked endless circles round the table and eight empty chairs.

In one sense the two ladies knew they weren't so very different themselves, although they pretended to be with their talk of London and fashion designers who were once well known and that coterie of accomplished painters the critics called the 'Glasgow Boys'. They were both unhappily – if hazily – aware of what was happening to them: that they were becoming afraid of real life and becoming more and more apart from it with the years. They never spoke of their shared fate: it was a truth too awful to encompass properly, encountered so late in the day as this, and neither of them dared to come too close to it, to hazard to that edge. So they held back and didn't speak of it and tried to appear content with the ritual as it had developed: continuing from week to week to steer the same wary circle around each other, forfeiting direct questions, working on instincts and imagined knowledge for the sake of harmony, each to preserve her own secrets, the little white lies.

Bizarrely it had taken them both a year and a half just to discover what the other's first name was. At last they'd found out an address too – extracted from countless hints and clues – and several times they'd individually tracked their way under cover of darkness and stood on mushy leaves under dripping trees in a sooty sandstone square to spy, but neither had invited the other to her home or could have contemplated it. There was a vague suggestion that Miss Caldwell's flat was filled with Hartnell and Balenciaga creations bought at cost price, and drawers of exotic turbans and gloves, and racks of shoes too good to soil on Glasgow's pot-holed streets; it was never established that on Miss McLeod's walls did *not* hang a gallery of inherited canvases by expensive artists which museums and salerooms would have fought with their claws to get hold of.

Miss Barclay's tea room closed when the tenement building was scheduled to come down, and they tried other places: a Scandinavian smörgåsbord room with dwarf log stools that gave them cramp, the Curler's Arms (nice, with wood fires – but sometimes there'd be a beery smell from the night before), then some of the little healthfood shops that opened up, which served thoughtful food but vile decaffeinated coffee with no taste. Miss McLeod suggested the Grosvenor Hotel on Great Western Road, and Miss Caldwell – anxious about the possible expense with the summer sales coming up – confected a tale she often repeated that season, to do with a man who'd once betrayed her by not showing up for a rendezvous. By way of reply Miss McLeod embellished a story about 'Alistair', who'd actually been her deceased sister's young man years ago, but it was left to Miss Caldwell to presume that *she* had been the object of his affections. 'Yes, I've had my chances all right,' they each told the other wistfully. And talked of Paris again – home of artistic genius and of Chanel's little black suit and that young whizz-kid Saint Laurent – and they agreed how wonderful it must be to live in such a place where romance was the very air you breathed.

Eventually, by mutual agreement, their two shared mornings a week were spent in the upstairs tea room in the Art Galleries, that awesome edifice with a silhouette like giant red sandstone sugar sifters. Getting there involved a hike across Kelvingrove Park, but the subsidized cost of the coffee meant more to Miss Caldwell than the price of Rayne's shoe leather and although Miss McLeod knew that little parties from her old school regularly paraded the galleries of sculpture and Impressionist masterpieces under the supervision of those pert young wives in polo-necks and sling-backs who made teachers nowadays and who'd taken her place, she felt the walk down past the Gothic university with its turrets and steeples, and the atmosphere of learning and 'mind' inside the Art Galleries somehow gave her a spiritual authority to compensate for her rather dowdy appearance, which no amount of effort seemed able to rectify.

They would amble round the exhibition rooms after their two coffees and one empire biscuit apiece. Miss Caldwell walked with majestic slowness and the semblance of keen attention – but didn't like to miss a chance to study herself in the glass panels in the frames. Miss McLeod screwed up her eyes behind her spectacles and memorized the artists' names on the plaques for later reference. In the French Room they stopped by the pretty Parisian views – Miss Caldwell (seeing through herself) claimed she liked the 'smudgy' Impressionist ones best, but wasn't able to remember a word of Miss McLeod's painstaking lectures from the times before, about the difference between Manet and Monet for instance. The two of them peered at Paris (Miss Caldwell carefully noting her reflection afloat over the images), they sat down on the benches to reflect, they grew almost tearfully nostalgic for the city neither had visited. (Now they each wished they hadn't confessed as much at the beginning but had left the matter open, as if it might seem they'd happened never to have mentioned the fact . . .)

One fateful day they stayed on for lunch in the Art Galleries and in the afternoon took the bus into town and went to the Glasgow Film Theatre (they preferred to call it by its former name, the Cosmo Cinema) and there (with OAP tickets) they settled down to watch 'The Umbrellas of Cherbourg', announced at the doors as part of something called a 'Jacques Demy Retrospective'. Cherbourg wasn't Paris, of course, but they'd come prepared to accept it as a substitute. Not that the closeness or not of the resemblance greatly concerned them when the lights dimmed in the over-heated auditorium. For they discovered with a most unpleasant shock that they weren't educated to suffer the conditions of modern film-watching. They didn't care for this seedy, heavy-breathing mid-afternoon clientèle, not one bit. Glasgow wasn't what it had been, they agreed in loud whispers. A woman with cropped hair wearing a black plastic jacket kept watching them, and a young couple in the darkness behind groaned grossly like animals. Miss Caldwell was too doubtful to venture into the 'Ladies' even and came out at the end feeling her finery was contaminated with the lives they'd been sitting so close to and also aware of a damp sensation at the tops of her legs; Miss McLeod emerged behind her into the cruel daylight of Sauchiehall Street, trembling like an aspen leaf, her legs scarcely able to support her, sick to the pit of her stomach, quite positive she'd recognized an old pupil at last, sitting in one of the rows in front with his arm wrapped caressingly around another man's shoulders.

1981's was a savage winter. Snow lay eighteen inches deep in Kelvingrove Park. Miss Caldwell in layers of outdated woollens huddled over a one-bar electric fire in her cavernous first-floor sitting room. Listening to the radio in her gaunt damp flat, Miss McLeod was almost sure she heard the announcer say the name of her teacher-friend who'd returned to Aberdeenshire when he read out a news item about a woman having been snowed in and dying in a blackout. With this terrible new sadness to bear and no way of confirming it (the newsagent's was at the world's end), she lost much of her own will to live this winter out.

Through the icy windows Huntly Gardens was like an Arctic wilderness, beyond saving. A pipe had burst in the kitchen, now another split in the bathroom; the gas went funny and wouldn't light, she ran out of matches to try; the radio battery faded to nothing, and she retired without hope to bed, her head humming with memories. She'd exhausted the supplies of food in her larder, was too proud to use her phone to summon help, and died of pneumonia and starvation in the course of three long days and nights when the snows blown from Greenland blizzarded across Glasgow's genteel West End and transformed it into a frozen beautiful winter composition by Sisley or Pissarro.

To Miss Caldwell's surprise, weeks after the funeral and when the last of the snow had melted away, an envelope embossed with the address of a lawyer's office dropped through her letter-box. She picked it up, turned it over. She braved the cold in the kitchen and made herself a cup of instant coffee – she didn't go out now, she'd forgotten the taste of the real thing – and she postponed opening the envelope till she'd extricated all the excitement she thought she could stand. When she slit the gummed flap with a knife and unfolded the letter inside to read it, she wasn't disappointed by its news. Coming quickly to the point, her correspondent informed her that, after numerous gifts to family cousins, Miss Elizabeth McLeod had stipulated in her will a bequest to be made to her for a sum of £500.

Two or three days later, when she'd recovered from the surprise, Miss Caldwell found her thoughts were turning again and again to an imagined version of Paris, which they'd spoken of so often and so fondly together. She even dreamed of the paintings in the galleries, sleeping slumped over her *Glasgow Herald*. She wondered once or twice if it could be a message from 'beyond'. Quite by chance she saw Perry Como on television singing 'April in Paris', and the same week a holiday programme did a feature on bargain spring holidays in the city.

One chilly morning with a blue sky she donned a turban (black, out of respect) and a heavy tweed coat (belted and edged with white fur on the cuffs, so very different from the one her late friend used to wear) and walked down busy Byres Road – taking constant note of the state of frost on the slippery pavements – to one of the travel agents. (I do it as my own tribute to a remembered friendship, she persuaded herself.) In the brochures the assistant gave her which she took back home to read, she thought everyone in the illustrations of Paris looked so young. There were hardly any elderly people at all to be seen. It concerned her a little bit that no one in the photographs wore the same sort of clothes as hers or appeared to take the pains about dressing that she did.

Another blue morning with another blue sky overhead she took a brisk walk to a smart little complex of mews shops behind Byres Road, with a purpose already fixed in her mind. It was spring sale time, and in one of the boutiques she knew what she would find: a rail of half-price couturier dresses. Inside, positioned at the rail, she only looked at the ones with Paris labels. She found those that were her own size and selected one in festive red jersey wool, with a pleated skirt and a gilt belt and a cowl neck to conceal her least flattering feature. In the mirror, walking like the restaurant mannequins of her working years, she thought they did each other justice, she and the dress. She was conscious of other shoppers interrupting their foraging just to look at her.

She paid for the dress and left the shop carrying it in a splendid silver-coloured plastic bag. On her way home she went into a building society office and opened an account for the £400 left from the lawyer's cheque. It would be a nice little nest egg, she told herself: something put away – plus interest. For a rainy day. For when the bills became even harder to pay. She reflected that sometimes – very occasionally – a little madness was permissible, like the dress: but prudence was safer, in the long run. Nest eggs and rainy days, for when the bills became headaches you went to bed with and woke up with. Such is life, being canny, sensible. If I doubt it, she explained to herself for consolation's sake, think of my friend Tilly McLeod, obviously so careful with her money.

Finishing her business in the building society, she noticed the cashier looking at the swanky bag. 'I'm going to a wedding,' she told him, unable to help herself.

She walked back outside through the revolving smoked glass doors, into what was left of the blue frosty morning, disturbed at her untruth. (Her radar set her on the right track home, and she walked automatically.) Even the sun shining now wasn't able to lift her spirits. Her good sense – the red dress and the lie about the wedding excepted – made her feel despondent. When on earth *would* she wear the dress?

Safely past the Grosvenor Hotel and temptation, her legs slowed. Suddenly she felt a panicky fear at the cargo in her bag; she *feared* it, the dress, wrapped like treasure in green tissue paper. (She wanted to smile and shrug her shoulders, she couldn't.) But what she feared even more she realized was still to come, and it was worse than dying in the street could be or hearing a ghost at her shoulder. She envied Tilly McLeod her escape, envied her it bitterly. Oblivion couldn't be worse than that ice-box bedroom at the back of the flat and the bleak lightbulb in the fringed shade.

Or maybe – could it have been – she'd intended to help her, her Tuesday and Friday friend whose appalling end had been reported on the front page of the *Herald*, the money gifted to her was supposed to be buying her some comfort?

She continued to walk but slowing her steps still more, to allow the thought to register. It was coming to her, as all important things had a way of doing, out of the blue. She took advantage of the pause to draw her breath and looked down at her silver carrier bag.

She was remembering something: waking in her armchair one night and hearing the man on the God-slot saying 'It's the mysteries that save us.'

Half-way along Grosvenor Terrace, in the middle of the pot-holed pavement, she stood considering the words. *It's the mysteries that save us.*

Would her friend have known and been able to tell her what the 'mysteries' were? Or could you only discover for yourself?

Did a 'mystery' need to be religious? What about – even –

pirouetting for the tarnished oval of mirror in the wardrobe: could that possibly count? Or having a catnap dream in her big comfy armchair? Looking at pretty, 'smudgy' pictures on a gallery wall? Joining in the silly words of a song and hearing Perry Como with a voice like maple syrup say it was called 'the cork-popping champagne city'?

DROWNING

Enid Gauldie

The camp lay at the foot of an acre of jungly raspberry canes, well away from the farmhouse. The lorry dropped us at the entrance to the stack yard and from there the farm grieve led Miss Harris and Miss Duncan ahead, pushing their cases on a handcart.

Miss Duncan was a strong and competent woman in her middle years, sensibly dressed for the country. It was difficult to believe she had ever thought of marriage. Miss Harris, younger only by a year or two, was in every way more frail. Her dress was a little too light, her court shoes too pretty, for the job in hand. Drifts of her fine hay-coloured hair escaped the fashionable snood into which she had tucked it. Her stocking seams wound crookedly up her thin calves.

We giggled softly, sad for her, because her petticoat hung down a trifle below her skirt hem.

'She's going with a Pole,' said Matty, who always knew.

'My Mum says she's missed the bus,' said Janet, whose mother always knew.

'My Dad says she's a dried up old maid,' said Isa.

Miss Harris was too evidently not dried up. She was liquid with hope, deliquescent with longing. She embarrassed us, our own anxieties just emerging.

We draggled behind, carrying our bags and parcels. It was like walking across a green sea to a new country, the raspberry bushes, tall on either side of the path, threatening to engulf us. Safe, everyday reality was left behind on the road. Camp life lay ahead.

We came to ten large wooden huts. Six of them had wooden beds built in tiers around their matchboard walls. The others housed dining hall, stores, latrines and cook house. Each sleeping hut had a little entrance porch, six by six, with a shelf at the side on which stood a white enamel basin with a navy blue rim and a large enamel jug. On the beds were billowing sacking mattresses stuffed with chaff, filling the air with the musty smell of new hessian and dusty barns. We had been told to bring our own sheets and pillowcases and our first task was to jump and roll on the mattresses until they were flattened enough to fit our bed linen. Pent up on the train, unsure of what lay ahead and most of us away from home for the first time, we had energy to spare for those mattresses and we pummelled them until the fine dust rising from them stifled us.

This isolated camp in the country had been built to house Free Polish soldiers, those who had escaped from their own invaded country and were gathering here to fight again. They had gone now to join British troops abroad and the huts had been swept and scrubbed clean of their presence. But we were aware of them, very aware. Living in their huts, sleeping in their beds, gazing at the same knot holes in the pine ceiling, we could hardly ignore them. Aloud we giggled about them, retelling the prevalent myths about the Poles, that they used scent, wore hairnets in bed, clicked their heels and bowed all the time.

But in the dark we thought about them, wondered what kind of beds they slept on now, how many of them were dead. We were a troop of women, fifty girls and their two guardian teachers, isolated from the war, from men and boys, a raft of women floating on a dark sea.

In the morning the grieve blew a cruel whistle to waken us. Then the cooks banged dustbin lids to let us know breakfast was ready. We ate at trestle tables, carrying there our own enamel mugs and plates and our own cutlery which afterwards we had to wash. Dazed still with sleep, we found communal breakfast unappealing and stuffed bread rolls into our pockets to eat at lousin' time.

Raspberry picking was the schoolchildren's contribution to the war effort. Farmers were shorthanded and politicians urged increased food production. Whatever Hitler did, the fruit still ripened and had to be picked and despatched to the jam factories. It was a trip away from home, a few shillings in our pockets, but the work was hard and the farmer relentless.

We wore our oldest clothes with sacking aprons tied over them. Each of us was provided with a 'luggie', a small, galvanized bucket which we attached to a piece of string tied round our waists. In the mornings pairs of girls were stationed at the ends of the rows of raspberry bushes, one at either side. When the whistle blew we began to pick berries, using both hands, dropping the berries into our luggies as fast as we could. At intervals along the rows were larger buckets, two for each girl. As our luggies filled we emptied them into the buckets, continuing the process until both large buckets were filled to the brim with squashy fruit. Then with a shout to our partners, 'I'm off to get weighed!', we dragged the heavy pails full of berries to the top of the field. On a wooden platform, raised up some three feet off the ground, the farmer's wife sat on an old kitchen chair, with darkened wooden barrels ranged beside her. As we heaved our buckets up on to the platform she emptied them into the barrels, giving us two pence out of her pinny pocket for each bucketful.

In some fields, where the berries hung thickest, we could earn our money easily, large ripe berries falling softly and quickly into our luggies. In others, where the ground was poorer or the bushes old, the berries were fewer and harder to find among the leaves, shrivelled and reluctant to leave their cores when our fingers pulled. Then it took a long time to make fourpence.

The money was not, for most of us, the prime reason for being in the berry fields. It was an outing, a holiday in the fresh air, an adventure. Wartime propaganda made us feel uplifted and virtuous for doing our bit, helping to beat Jerry, fighting on the home front. To aid our feeling of being at war we had all, by one means or another, kitted ourselves out with trousers of sorts, old washed-out mechanics' dungarees, brothers' hand-me-down grey flannels, land army breeches. Girls in the 1940s did not wear trousers unless they were in the Services. We felt released by those trousers from all kind of feminine restraints. No need to worry about skirts riding up, knickers and stocking tops showing. The freedom with which we could lift a leg over a fence or climb into a lorry made us new people, free of our mothers, free of school.

Even the labour, and the consequent tiredness, meant a kind of freedom. We all came from modest, respectable homes, sheltered from the harder world of really poor children. It was a new feeling to be tired by a day's work. We picked and carried berries till our legs and shoulders ached. Our arms, growing browner each day, were scratched from wrist to elbow by the thorny branches and rough leaves. The pale undersides of raspberry leaves have a texture like sandpaper, bristled over with a thousand microscopic hooklets. Our necks and faces were bitten by berry bugs. Our fingers were stained purple with raspberry juice and our clothes were stiff with it. At night when we shut our eyes raspberries swam in swarms behind our eyelids, shifting in scarlet patterns. We swooned and drowned in shattered crimson light.

In the fields there was one world, fenced in by the rows of bushes, the horizon always invisible, our own companions cordoned beside us, in camp another world, just as confined. There was no wireless, we saw no newspapers, we floated away from the war. We lived in a country of women, a world wholly unfeminine because it was hard, outdoor, rough living and yet somehow we were all more tremblingly aware of being female.

The worst camp task, one at which we were all forced to take a turn, was the twice-weekly emptying of the waist-high oil can of used sanitary towels. It had to be carried from the latrines to the cookhouse furnace and there tipped into the flames. The smell, a mixture of chlorine disinfectant and stale, dried blood was overwhelming. We shrank away from it. It took two of us to carry the heavy can and we walked, our faces turned away from the contents and from each other, hoping not to be seen in the act, even by our friends. Men faced with dirty tasks make coarse humour out of it, loud with bravado. We never spoke, never mentioned the duty to each other. We tried to dissociate ourselves from it altogether, not admitting even to ourselves that we bled, as all women bleed.

The only men we saw during the weeks we stayed in the camp were the bad-tempered old grieve and the tinkers. In the trees beyond the fields the tinkers camped every summer for the berry season, had done from time immemorial, do so still. The Townsleys, the M'Larens and the Lees gathered together from all over Scotland for the picking. They built their round, primeval huts, of tarpaulin over bent willow cane, on the same sites every year. The grass never grew on the round, ashy places where they built their fires. The farmer set them to pick in fields away from us, keeping them separate, as they always had been. They were quiet and decent people, working hard and giving no trouble, but they looked like desperadoes, not Aryan and dark like Romanys, but flat-faced and red-haired, aboriginal. Their children were filthy and dressed in rags, and they ducked away as if too accustomed to violence. They were mostly women and children, their menfolk, like ours, away to the war, but there was a coven of adolescent boys who made us uneasy. They never cat-called or whistled like the boys we knew at home but they lurked. Their walk was springy and hang-dog at the same time, as if holding something threatening in check.

Although safe from them, in fact quite unthreatened, we were aware of them, just as we were, always, aware of those absent Polish soldiers.

There came a spell of burning weather. We sweated in the dusty fields, beating off the flies. The paths between the berry bushes dried out hard underfoot. Over the bitumen roofs of the huts breathed a haze of heat. At night, in our prickly beds, the little, hard edges of dry chaff pushing through the sheets, we scratched. Our skin, roughened and tanned, felt unfamiliar to our fingertips.

One evening Miss Harris and Miss Duncan, watching us limping home, too hot and tired for our usual fooling, offered to take us swimming. There was a little loch nearby, they said. We could walk over there after tea. No swimming costumes? It didn't matter. No one ever came there. We could swim in our knickers. Giggling, we washed for supper and, hurrying for once through the cardboardy pies full of gristle and the grey, sodden potatoes, were waiting to be led to the water.

It was so short a distance from the camp, we were surprised not to have known of its existence. Lying under a hill's shadow, closed in by willows and alder, the loch water lay green and silver, reflecting the trees and the evening sky. All round the edge were slatey stones greened over with algae, with cushioned islands of moss among them. Reedy shallows lay between the stony, sloping beach and the deeper water, the bottom shelving suddenly beyond the reeds. Fronds of a feathery, drifting weed clogged the surface and clung round the swimmers' ankles. We shrieked and grabbed each other, splashing showers of water that seemed dense and silvery like mercury. Feeling the wetness on our unwashed, dried-out skin, we were transported.

After the first, lively, splashing about we quietened down, floating in dreamlike suspension on the warm, thick water. Time passed unnoticed until the light slipped away behind the hill. The greens and silvers dulled. Arms lifted above the water grew goose pimples. Miss Harris and Miss Duncan, waiting on the beach with towels, called us in to the shore. They had become aware of a group of tinker boys in the trees. 'Go round behind the bushes, girls, and dress quickly,' said Miss Duncan briskly, making light of it. She walked over towards the trees to warn the boys off while Miss Harris hovered over us as if she could shelter our semi-nakedness with her own spare body.

We rubbed ourselves with our thin wartime towels and dressed hurriedly, glancing always over our shoulders, like frightened birds feeding. In a moment Miss Duncan came back, panting.

'There's been an accident,' she cried. 'Those stupid boys didn't know what to do. They were frightened to tell us. I've sent them off for help but I'd better go to the phone myself.'

Time slowed down and the light ebbed gently, reluctantly. Clouds of evening birds whistled as they passed overhead with a riffling breath of wings. We stood about, not sure what we were waiting for. Miss Harris and Miss Duncan bustled from loch's edge to field path, looking for, expecting what?

After a time there came an organized group, two ambulance men with stretcher poles, the farmer and his wife showing the way, a doctor with a Gladstone bag, the grieve in waders, and behind them, like whipped dogs, the tinker boys. They moved about in front of us in an absurd charade, with much gesture and posturing, much pointing and changing of position. Eventually two of the boys, grown bolder, dared to talk to the grieve. With a backward glance at us, stripping off jackets, shirts and shoes, they sped, surprisingly expert, into the now dark water. Casting about in the very spot where we, so short a time ago, had floated, they dipped below the surface, thin feet threshing, searching among the clinging bottom weeds.

And, in a while, they brought him up, a limp, drowned boy, all white and silver. Dripping green tendrils of weed spilled from his head so that he seemed to have green hair. His silvered skin gleamed in the thin light. He seemed not so much dead as never human. We had never seen a naked boy before, or a dead one. As we watched him borne away we thought how we had swum in the water over him, his white body lying underneath us as we floated, separated from him only by the same shifting element that had killed him.

WHEN
THE HARD RAIN FALLS

Alan D. Kerr

The city-bound train huffs round the curve and into the station. I clamber into a compartment in the leading carriage, clunking the door shut behind me. Sitting opposite a red-headed girl, I open my briefcase and take out a slim volume entitled *Sight-reading for Schools*, which I begin to peruse as we set off clickety-clack along the track. Concentration is difficult, what with the racketing of the train and the temptation to steal a peek at the girl who, I notice, is immodestly showing off the bare skin at the top of her stockings.

CORKERHILL. SHIELDS ROAD. The stations come and go, the distance between them so short that the lumbering locomotive hardly has time to pick up speed leaving one before it trundles into the next. I close the book. What's the point? If I don't know it now, I never will.

The train has stopped again. CUMBERLAND STREET. Beneath the nameboard on the station building some hand has scrawled MENTAL CUMBIE ROOLZ OKAY in spidery letters. Somewhere a whistle blows, and we're on our way, chuffing towards St Enoch's.

As I'm cramming the book back into my briefcase, a city gent opposite straightens out his newspaper and an ominous headline captures my eye: KENNEDY ORDERS ARMS BLOCKADE OF CUBA. US READY TO SINK SOVIET SHIPS.

Ten o'clock. In the musicroom Mr Wood kicks off with sight-reading. The first boy he puts through his paces dithers on a doh, falters on a fah, so meets with the rough justice dispensed to those whose performance falls short of the target. Thwack! Thwack! Thwack! Thwack! Four of the best! I sit trying to control the butterflies that swarm in my stomach, finding some small consolation in the notion that my achievement of 100 per cent in last term's music exam may have lengthened the odds against being asked to perform. Every Good Boy Deserves Favour!

Lunchtime. Munchtime. I beat a path for the lunchroom. On entering, I spot my classmate Prof McDougall, and sit beside him. Prof knows all there is to know about anything (except girls) and then some. The class brainbox. I greet him.

'Hiya Prof!'

'Hello,' says he. I pour some creamy tomato soup from my flask, and take a roll and sausage with beetroot out of my Tupperware box. We eat in silence.

Twisting the soup-stained cup back on my flask, it occurs to ask Prof's opinion of the headline I'd seen earlier in the day.

'Prof, you had a swatch at this morning's paper?'

'Yep.'

'What d'you make of the Cuban carry-on?' He takes his time answering. His eyes screw up in the characteristic way he has when thinking hard. It's almost as if being brainy hurts.

'Cuba. Hmmm . . . kind of serious if you ask me.'

'How serious?' Another screwed-up face.

'Very. In fact, it could start a nuclear war, and that might be rather nasty.'

'Who for?'

'All of us.'

'Och, you're kidding. It's between the Yanks and the Russkies isn't it? Nothing to do with us.'

'Yep, but don't forget the Yanks've a nuclear submarine base on the Clyde.'

After lunch I pay a visit to the school library, virtually deserted as I make my way to the General Reference section. I soon find what I'm looking for. *Encyclopaedia Britannica.* I select a volume, and sandwiched between NOVOSIBIRSK and NUCLEIC ACID discover NUCLEAR FISSION.

I seem to float through the afternoon in a sort of haze. Double

French looms up first. All my mind wants to do is indulge in bi-lingual morbidity:

'*Qu'est-ce que c'est?*'

'*C'est un Apocalypse!*'

Then double Geography. Today's topic, Physical Geography. Mr Cotter distributes Ordnance Survey maps of Glasgow. In thirty seconds I pinpoint my street, familiar landmarks. The railway. The cemetery. A shiver ripples down my spine. Then teacher's voice penetrates the mist. I try hard to pay attention. My neighbour nudges my elbow and motions towards the rear of the class. There, I see two boys studiously exploring the contours of each other's manhood. Physical Geography!

The day ends with Maths. If only I could understand what Mr Halley is talking about, it would help my concentration. But no. Imagination gets the upper hand. Sir mentions a vector, and in my mind's eye appears an earnest Irish policeman, bawling into his two-way radio: 'This is Z Vector 1 to BD. Listen, there's absolute bloody chaos here at the Civil Defence dug-out. People fightin' tooth and nail to get in. I don't think I can control the situation much longer!'

'BD to Z Vector 1. There's only one thing for it. Use the gun you've been issued. Over and out!'

At long last four o'clock. As I cross the playground heading for the main gate, I bump into Charlie Wilson from 4C. He lives near me, and decides to join me on the train home. We clear the school precincts, cut across George Square and into Queen Street. Halfway down, we stop, dump our schoolbags on the pavement, and begin pointing at the guano-streaked heights of a building. Our ruse has the desired effect. Passers-by look skywards. Satisfied, we walk on. Down into Argyle Street, strangely quiet without the trams.

With a minute to spare, we board the train. Charlie immediately swings into action, wedging his executive-style briefcase against the doorhandle in such a way that no one can enter the compartment. We settle down to a king-size cigarette as the train starts to move, Charlie lounging at length on his four seats, me on mine. Charlie has been known to occupy the luggage-rack. I open the conversation.

'Charlie.'

'Check.'

'How d'you feel about being wiped out?' Silence. I look over to see him blow a huge smoke ring which curls sluggishly towards the ceiling.

'Wiped out,' he says eventually. 'You mean at the bookies, like?'

'No. I mean being burnt to a frazzle in a nuclear war.'

'Who said anything about a nuclear war for Chrissake?'

'Don't you read the papers Charlie?'

'*Sporting Life* now and again.' Charlie inhabits a world of his own. A world of trebles, accumulators, short heads and long odds. Maybe I should try another tack.

'Charlie.'

'Check.'

'What'd you do if you found out you'd only twenty-four hours to live?'

'That's dead easy. Have it away with every girl in sight.'

'Listen . . . you ever . . . you know, made love?'

'Check.'

I arrive home to find my mother and grandmother in the living room, drinking tea and chatting. I join them, and Granma asks how I'm getting on at school. Terrific. She takes out her purse, the Tuesday ritual, hands me half-a-crown, and urges me not to spend it all in one shop. I swallow a cup of tea, then my mother tells me to go and get on with my homework. Climbing the stairs to the first landing, I wonder about the relevance of homework, of school, of anything. Come the mushroom cloud most things will be academic.

I call in at the toilet, do a job, and remain seated on the porcelain throne trying to marshal my thoughts. I mean, where have I been, what have I seen? What to show for sixteen and a bit years of living? Not a lot. And worst of all. I've never made love. Not once.

After tea, I try to settle with my homework, but somehow fail to see the point. And my mind keeps flipping back to the TV news I'd seen before coming up to my room. Pictures of US warships on station. Snatches of commentary – 'Tanks and troops out in Havana . . . country on war footing . . . White House taking a firm stand.'

I admit defeat, go downstairs to the hall, and dial my girl-friend's number. She answers.

I say: 'Hiya Margaret, it's me. Listen, you doing anything tonight?'

'Baby-sitting for my mum. She's away to *Five Past Eight* at the Alhambra.'

'I see. Okay if I come round?'

'If you like.' I like. Before leaving the house I have a wash, put on my best shirt and the psychedelic tie my globe-trotting uncle brought from Honolulu.

As I tramp up the hill towards the flats where Margaret lives, a muffled crowd-roar swells in the distance. Can't be Ibrox. Not on a Tuesday night. Maybe a meet at the White City. Funny name for a greyhound track. White City. Sounds more like an Arabian Nights city, shimmering dazzlewhite in the hot haze of a desert noon.

In front of the flats I encounter a drunk who wants to be pally.

'Hullawrer son,' he drawls. I try to circumnavigate but, persistent, he catches my arm.

'Yawright son,' he goes on.

'Fine.'

'An' tell mi son, wheryigaun?'

'To see my girlfriend.'

'Heh, a wee date. Rats magic. Ah've goat a date too son . . . wi' oblivion.'

Margaret opens the door, still dressed in her school uniform. We go into the lounge, and I sit close to her on the settee. The TV is on. Emergency Ward 10.

After some smalltalk, I decide to take the bull by the horns.

'Margaret.'

'Yes.'

'I want to ask you something . . . important.'

'What's that?'

I know what I want to say, but the words play hide-and-seek. My mouth is dry, my palms sweaty.

'Come on then. What is it?' she says.

It's now or never.

'Margaret, can I . . . I . . . make love to you?'

A pregnant pause. Then she says: 'Aren't you supposed to work up to it, get in the mood. I mean, it's not very romantic just coming straight out with it.'

'Please.'

'I don't think I'm ready. Maybe later.'

'But Margaret, there may not be a later. The Third World War's about to start. We may not survive the next few days.'

'You mean because of Cuba?'

'Yes.' I stroke her hair gently with my hand. I want to say more, but the moment seems somehow magic. Margaret breaks the silence, and the spell.

'You honestly believe there may be a war?'

'It's funny. Part of me says the idea's ridiculous, there's too much to lose. But another part, deep down, says it might just happen.'

'Oh God,' she whispers, then starts to sob, She turns to me and looks into my eyes, tears streaming down her face.

'Do you love me?'

'Of course I do.'

She gets up, goes over to the coffee table, pulls a tissue out of a box, then wipes away her tears.

'D'you fancy a drink?'

I say yes, and she pours herself a vodka, whisky for me, from the cabinet over by the window. We sit on the settee, hand in hand, sipping in silence. Her drink finished, she puts her glass on the floor and starts to unbutton her blouse.

'Please be gentle,' she says.

THE MINISTER'S WIFE

Morag MacInnes

Mrs Murison does all that is expected of her and more. Everybody says that. Nobody is the least grudging with their praise – nobody, that is, on the periphery. Within the church community it is different, of course – families, traditionally, see the warts and all. Well-intentioned onlookers are much too sorry for her to criticize – the casual sort of people who come in to help with jumble sales at the last minute, or give the odd talk to the Guides about wholefoods, contraception or carpentry. Every mother in the town knows that the Bluebells, White Heathers and Daffodils call her Dreary, not Deirdre, which is her proper name. They also know that the Guides are fed-up with wholefoods, contraceptives and carpentry, and would much rather have patrol competitions about Uniforms Past and Present, which is the sort of thing they used to get with Miss Ledbetter. However, she's dead, old Ledbelly, khaki knickers and all (those last, with the pink elastic stockings, made camp-fire cocoa a treat; she squatted square on her collapsible stool, like an elevated bullfrog; the circle of firelit faces showed collective awe). Mrs Deirdre Murison does her bit instead, and believes very much in being modern and psychological about it all, and the mothers know better than to interfere. Somebody in the community has got to be earnest, they suppose; who better than the minister's wife?

She does not receive the same kind of tolerance from her husband's flock. They are of course aware of the Reverend's views, and conclude for the most part that he's young and will learn: but when Deirdre popped her head up and announced at the sewing circle that she was absolutely in accord with Derek's sermon last week about Relevance, and what did everybody think about arms control, they were a little agitated. A wife, they felt, should gently steer her husband away from excesses, of whatever sort. Deirdre is not perhaps as suitable as she might be . . . but, as Mrs Hamilton has been heard to remark, after a satisfying evening demonstrating her string and pin hangings, you're a long time in the Manse. The ladies of Drysdale Church of Scotland are biding their time despite the implication, hovering angel-like above their heads, that Jesus might not approve of the Tory party, and might even have doubts about the SDP. They are well aware that Deirdre's pedigree is impeccable – you can tell by looking at her. She looks like a woman who has always done all that's expected of her and more. She and Elijah, the Manse dog, share the same large brown eyes and hopeful lift of the chin. You feel you wouldn't be surprised to find a tail lurking as well, aching to wag, if you were to ferret – awful thought – among her sensible M & S underthings. Her skin is pale, her forehead creased with good intentions: she comes from a Church of Scotland minister's family, and the modest tallow-candle look is there, no matter what she does with perms and gypsy hoops and the odd spot of make-up. Somehow, in the 1960s, when she was having her rebellious phase (so useful, it turned out to be, when trying to cope with the Guides who tore out the Commissioner's tent pegs in a thunderstorm) – somehow, her caftan always looked newly washed: she wandered about Edinburgh in an opera cloak, floppy blue hat and cow-bells, like part of a school crocodile separated from the main body. Now she wears lots of jumble sale clothes of necessity, not choice, and has discovered to her chagrin that the other young mums wouldn't touch them with a bargepole – not to *wear* – so she is out of step again. Still, she does her best. She has always admired her husband and the strength of his commitment to what he calls a vital rejuvenation, a revolutionary re-assessment of his Church and its affairs. Red wine at the Church social, he assures her, is just the thin edge of the wedge. He's persuasive, tireless, *engagé*: he is from a new mould. Deirdre has always been very proud of him.

In a way it's a pity they've landed in Drysdale. It's a

beautiful little place near enough Edinburgh for Deirdre to be able to pop in and visit her mum in Morningside most week-ends: she piles the kids in the back of the Mini – Elijah stays home because of hairs – and blithely sets off. Her mother makes her garage the car, because she finds Derek's CND stickers lacking in dignity and doesn't see why she should inflict them on her neighbours. (She hasn't actually said all this; Deirdre just knows. There is often a gap between what Deirdre's mother says, especially about Derek, and what she thinks. Deirdre understands and respects this, her mother's brand of tolerance.) It's good to be so near the city, yet still in pretty countryside with nice old pubs and most of the original village still intact, huddled round Derek's fine grey kirk. The only trouble is that Drysdale hasn't got a vital, rejuvenated, commit-ted church congregation. Rather the reverse. Out of that fine grey kirk, on the first Sunday morning in spring, a bonnie blue Scottish morning with a hint of frost in the air and the first snowdrops sheltering among the gravestones, will come only a handful of people, mostly elderly, mostly ladies, well protected from the canny blasts which assail them both inside and outside the church by furs and ferocious hats. It's a suburb of Edin-burgh; the rich live here and commute, or are retired, enjoying the fruits of their labours. In short, the young mums may drop by for a glass of wine but it is the rich Tory ladies who are the backbone of the Church. Fortunately for Derek he is young and looks, if not quite handsome, then vigorous; he has a way with the ladies. They will do a great deal for him; things they would certainly not do for his wife.

At the beginning of the year, the Drysdale Women's Institute adopted an African village. Derek, being strong on deprivation and the Third World, suggested it to Deirdre who was begin-ning to feel stifled by string and pin hangings and knitted squares. He could quite see, he said, why she should feel a little despairing; the answer was to make the Institute ladies relate to poverty on a one-to-one basis, if possible. He did not seem to think that this might be a particularly tall order; on the contrary, he said, it was exactly the kind of challenge a committed Christian could really get his teeth into. Or her teeth. Deirdre was with him absolutely as far as the poverty problem was concerned; deprivation, malnutrition, ignorance appal her. She sees them vividly, the poor black children, queuing for tin cans of water, never getting the right injections, carrying their bellies like pregnant women. They are not a media cliché for her: she is caught between tears of rage and frustration as she dumps débris from some coffee morning in the pig bin. Theoretically, idealogically speaking, she was all for the scheme. Practically speaking, however, she had some ignoble reservations.

Picture, if you can, an Institute meeting. There sits Mrs Hamilton, wrestling these days with macramé since one can only go so far with string and pin; her friend Miss MacPhee is at her side. They still enjoy their game of golf, these two; they are as weatherbeaten and formidable as Edinburgh Castle at sunset (their battlements are quite remarkable) and they are worth, taken together, a tidy sum. Mrs Dalzeil, the bank manager's wife, always attends; she is another modestly self-satisfied product of the Calvinist work ethic; she has an air of virtuous frugality and expensive bridgework. Gregor never lets me skimp on mechanics, she once told Deirdre, who had dropped in to ask if she could borrow the back garden again for the Guide camp. (No trouble, Mrs Dalzeil had said; just give me time to shift the horses.) On the other hand there is Mrs Philipson-Fordyce, who is divorced, and therefore Has a Past. She imparts a certain raffish flamboyance to the meetings – she is known to have entertained people from the BBC to weekend parties, and may not have earned her worldly rewards quite virtuously. She is not at all oatmeal brose-ish, like Mrs Dalzeil, more like pink salmon on crushed ice and you'd better not ask how she managed to get hold of it. Deirdre does not know which lady distresses her most. And those are just the tip of the Drysdale iceberg. Between them they could buy several African villages without getting a reproving letter from the bank; a century ago they'd have been out there enlightening the natives, to further the honour of the little lady who loved Balmoral (apart from Mrs Philipson-Fordyce, who would have been selling them gin into the bargain). They tolerate Derek; he can get conscience money out of them – he has charm. Deirdre has no charm; it was not, genealogically speaking, to the fore in her family. She is also the wrong sex. So, though she was absolutely in accord with Derek and believed in helping the rich to come to terms with their responsibility to the Third World, she quailed before this Amazonian assembly, stalwart offsprings of prudent Scottish Presbyterianism that they were. She developed the determined tone and resigned shoulder-line which characterizes members of the caring professions. Derek was being true to his Holy Ghost; he was building a billiard table with the young unemployed. She had to do her bit, and damned her reservations as timidity of spirit.

The Institute ladies received the Mbindera-Mbindu project with guarded enthusiasm. Derek, supportive as always, counselled and consoled his wife. He pointed out that true egalitarian crusading Christian charity could only come from within; it was only by identifying closely with the people of . . . whatsitsname? . . . that they could ever accept responsibility for the dispossessed of the world. Once her ladies got really involved, he assured her, they'd start to care. 'We have to personalize suffering,' he said. 'That makes it real.' So Deirdre made lists, planned fund raising events; she sent lots of questions out to their contact in Mbindera-Mbindu, the local teacher – questions all thought up by the Institute ladies. She asked for pictures, descriptions, information on all sorts of things. She took books on Africa out of the library and gave an introductory talk on the climate, geography and politics of the region. Her first few meetings were a modest success; the donations remarkably encouraging. Impetus was gathering nicely; she only wished the schoolteacher would write.

When he did, she tried hard not to be disappointed. She pinched herself sharply to remind herself of Derek's wise words about European Expectations and Colonial Arrogance. Perhaps she had expected too much. There was a grubby black and white photograph of mud huts; a few sad, incurious faces squinted at the camera. One woman held a child; it was impossible to tell whether her bunched and bundled cotton shift was gay and colourful, as Deirdre's books had said it would be, or not. The woman's face was impenetrably black. Moreover, the teacher was no letter writer. He answered each question, as it were, monosyllabically. Families? Twenty. Occupations? Varied. Climate? Hot and wet. Vegetation? Plentiful. It was hardly enough to go on. Deirde pushed away feelings of panic, and reminded herself that the poor man hadn't the least reason to sound anything other than matter-of-fact. His name was Mr Abong Mbang, and in the photograph he stood outside his school, his face disappearing into the shadow of the veranda. There was no glint of smiling teeth.

To keep the interest up, that was the problem. Deirdre's ladies, accustomed as they were to detailed and complicated soap opera, whether it was on telly, amongst royalty, or in their own village, couldn't be expected to take to Plentiful Vegetation and Various Occupations. Personalize it, Derek had said. Make them care for the people, then we'll introduce the ideas. Deirdre spent several weeks waiting for the postman, gazing over her dismal lumpy garden; then she resolved, almost with relief, to take matters into her own hands. Where the reports she had were scanty, she embroidered, improvised, expanded; when interest at the Institute meetings flagged, she introduced new developments in the life of Mbindera-Mbindu . . . small crises, little family tragedies. While her children were at school and Derek was discussing the psychological effects of long-term unemployment at the Community Centre, or composing a series of dialogues between God and a feminist for thought-provoking Sunday sermons, Deirdre sat at her formica-top table in the kitchen and prepared monthly reports on the distant, uncommunicative village. Despite herself, it seemed, they grew more and more . . . colourful. She herself couldn't have told you exactly when she passed the invisible divide between a forgivable attempt to pad out her information and an unforgivable lurch into the realms of pure fantasy. Perhaps the children pushed her over. When the long-awaited school photograph arrived, she furnished each anonymous anxious black face with a history. It was, fortunately, a small class; her imagination hardly faltered. She scored a palpable hit. The offspring of the Institute ladies, the young Hamiltons and Dalzeils and Philipson-Fordyces, were on the whole something of a disappointment to their parents. They were no longer the prepossessing sights they had once been, out for a walk in the Botanics dressed up in their kilts, or snug in those fine warm woolly coats with the velvet collars. They had grown up and away, and either curried favour, with an eye to their recession-hit bank balances, or saw their begetters as seldom, and as briefly, as possible. Deirdre's simple little tales awakened in her ladies deep nostalgia for the old, never-had-it-so-good days when their families were young and, generally speaking, bidd-able – and with the nostalgia came sentimentality, great profit-able gobbets of it. They simply could not hear enough about the children. Deirdre had hit the jackpot; she was forced to go into Edinburgh specially – the local library had given her all the help it could. 'Poor things,' muttered Mrs Hamilton, peering at a subdued pair holding hands in the bottom lefthand corner of the snapshot. 'Imagine having a witch doctor for a father. You wonder what he does if his rain spells don't work . . . that sort of frustration often vents itself at home, I've found . . .' Deirdre, while assuring her of Umboko's perfect familial devotion, found herself wondering whether witch doctors had families at all. Perhaps they're chaste, she thought, like monks? To strengthen the spells? Mrs Hamilton, contented, scanned the photo, fixing names to faces with the help of the minister's wife. She didn't doubt Deirdre's word. None of them did. They did not, after all, except to be led up the garden path; they expected Deirdre, despite her peculiarities, to be fundamentally decent. When Deirdre said the village needed a proper water supply, several of the ladies brought out their cheque books . . . She felt an uneasy elation, and after they had left, after she had emptied the chocolate crispie crumbs into the pig bin, she noted down the remarks she remembered making about the children. It would not do to become confused. She pinned a little bulletin up on the church notice board, with extra little snippets of news and gossip – only extrapolating, she told herself. Only expanding Mr Mbang's courteous, completely barren little communications. It was all in a good cause.

It could have gone on indefinitely. Why not? Except that one spring day Derek, popping into the kitchen for his elevenses, found his wife, not hovering over the tea cups or arranging the biscuits as usual, but gazing absently out of the window, as if the return of spring brought her nothing. He made no comment; he is a magnanimous man. He plugged the kettle in himself, and read Mr Mbang's latest letter while the water boiled. It seemed he was coming to Britain. Very soon, too; it was all quite unexpected. Deirdre said, rather crossly Derek thought, that Mr Mbang didn't look, from his photograph, like a man who would leap continents without a hint dropped, without notice given. Poor Deirdre. He would be staying for some time – learning about irrigation and soil science. A charity was paying his fees. He also said that he very much looked forward to meeting the kind ladies in Drysdale Women's Institute. Derek suggested a dinner dance in the golf club, to celebrate, and wondered a little at his wife's silence. His tea was much too strong, and he took it into his study and fed it to the geranium.

Deirdre was aware not so much of turmoil as of a deep, painful embarrassment. Derek would not understand. They had always believed in sharing (they had decided years ago that if Derek was attracted to someone else he would tell her immediately) – but she simply could not share this. It all had such a gradual build-up, she thought, rehearsing possible phrases – it's really terribly difficult to describe to someone else how it happened – you could hardly call what I did lying . . . but she knew that the minister could and would. So, more to the point, would the black school teacher, whom Deirdre had provided with two wives, several children, and a choleric temperament. Cold and lonely in the failing light from the kitchen window, she made a decision. Usually she addresses both God and Derek with childlike ease about everything from card tables to terrorists; this time she took advice from no one. She would have to throw herself upon the mercy of Mr Mbang; it was quite impossible for her to do anything else.

Mr Mbang in the flesh was of course nothing like his photograph. He was very small and dignified, and a matt black, not shiny. Deirdre did not like to peer too closely, in case she seemed to stare, but she thought she caught a hint of irony in his glance. Perhaps he was a bit cynical of all the do-gooders? (Derek had said Deirdre must be ready to accept this, so of course she was.) She was in a pitiable state of nerves when they met, in the golf club reception room; she showed her teeth too much – indeed, she could scarcely drag her lips over them, they felt so dry, like rough stones. Derek did not find her fixed rabbit stare appealing, and sent her anxious messages from across the room with his eyebrows. She grinned back, gummily. He had to ring round some of the young unemployed – they promised to provide music for the dance, and they were late. So he slipped out, leaving Deirdre alone with Mr Mbang for the first time. It was the moment she had been dreading. She had to explain to him how her best intentions had led her, somehow, into trouble. She clenched her fists, drew in a whisper of breath – and discovered that to confess was quite impossible. He would think she had been making a joke, a game, of his villagers. He said gently – perhaps he had noticed how scared she was – 'I do not know what is expected of me here, Mrs Murison. I am not a speechifier, not in the least. Perhaps you will be kind enough to guide me through the evening?'

Deirdre tried. She explained that he would make no speeches, just chat informally to her ladies. She would be close at hand all the time. 'You may find they have some . . . misconceptions,' was all she could bring herself to say. Then, after the chat, they'd have dinner, and then . . . 'Of course,' said Deirdre, 'you needn't stay for the dance bit at all, if you don't want to . . .'

'But I shall,' Mr Mbang said gravely. 'I shall be delighted to. Let us begin, then, with your ladies.' Presented with his tasks in order, he was as solemn as a schoolboy, and looked as though he meant to be thorough. Deirdre's tallowy forehead gleamed with despair as she began the introductions. Recklessly (what could it matter now?) she told Mr Mbang that Mrs Hamilton was particularly interested in voodoo, and retreated into a corner, where she waited miserably for the world to fall on her head.

She heard Derek summoning them all to the buffet, banging his spoon on the table in a bright, jolly, peremptory fashion, like a scout banging a bean pot, she thought, and her ladies left Mr Mbang abruptly. The guest of honour offered her his arm on the way into dinner, with perfect courtesy, and sat beside her. He enjoyed his wine. Well into the second course he turned to her. 'I am not married,' he said, 'but I am honoured that you thought I might be.' Was he being ironic? She couldn't tell, and blushed miserably. It occurred to her that God's face in judgement must be unreadable, like Mr Mbang's; an identifiable expression would seem much too domestic and reassuring. She waited. She would feel so much better once she had been reprimanded.

'There is nothing there, you know; no bright colours, or singing. Just sickness and hunger and heat. There is not enough of life left for it to become gossipy and inconsequential. It is boring, boring, boring – waiting for water, waiting for doctors, waiting for trucks to come.' Could Mrs Hamilton hear? She was so near; her cutlery squeaked on the plate at Deirdre's elbow. It had an impatient sound; Mrs Hamilton really preferred to use her fingers on a leg bone. The whites of Mr Mbang's eyes weren't white, Deirdre noticed helplessly: they were yellow. He was watching Mrs Hamilton, reflectively, as he spoke. 'We do not even tell stories to the children; we only watch for when they will be too ill to brush off the flies. Stories are no comfort; we are past needing them. But I can see why you do . . .' Mrs Philipson-Fordyce was picking her teeth; surreptitiously her enamelled nail rooted around her gums. Mrs Dalzeil's bridge-work was impenetrable but her knobbly chest shone with chicken grease. Miss MacPhee risked an elegant rift, a coy shiver of chins, behind her hand. '. . . Yes. So I told them all stories too. Just like you. *National Geographic, Readers' Digest* –

silly stories, like yours were. To keep them interested. To get their money. There is more than one way' – he smiled at her – 'to skin a crocodile. We are indeed partners in crime. But you mustn't feel bad about it, you know' (for Deirdre, red-cheeked, was about to pour out her guilt in a relieved rush of words). 'It's the end result which matters. Understanding takes much too long. You and I, we know that. We take short cuts. It's the practical thing to do.'

That was the end of the matter for him. He did not prolong things by asking Deirdre's opinion; he assumed her complicity, turned from her and paid elegant court to the ladies on the other side, telling them about bread-fruit pies, and coconut milk and roast yams. It was hardly a sweet reprieve. Unable to deliver her parcel of guilt and apology, Deirdre felt it weigh heavily on her hands and on her heart.

When Derek spoke later, in bed, about the evening she was irritable with him and wouldn't compose herself obligingly, spoon-fashion, for sleep, but lay on her back with her elbows stiff. He had only said that his next thought-provoking sermon might take as its subject Bridges – between Male and Female, Black and White, God and Man. 'Of course, I'll use your village . . . personalize it, that's the ticket. I bet Mrs H. isn't sleeping quite so easy in her bed tonight, not now that she's made contact with the poor.' Deirdre knew, alas, that Mrs H. was dreaming of lethal long black spears and hypnotic tribal rhythms. She felt lonely, being no longer innocent.

She does all that is expected of her and more, the minister's wife: she's a good hard-working girl – but she does seem a little glum, these days, a touch listless. There is not the same glowing, earnest eagerness in that pale face. Perhaps, think the Institute ladies, she's pregnant again.

THE SHOES

Brian McCabe

Archie Newton lifted out the inner bag, then undid the packet and flattened it out on the kitchen table. He laid one of his shoes on top, then drew a line around its sole with a biro. He did this twice on one side of the packet, then he turned it over and did the same with the other shoe. He sat down and started cutting out the foot-shaped pieces of cardboard. He looked at the clock on the kitchen windowsill, but he wasn't sure if the time it told was the right time. It was the same little square blue clock his mother had once tried to brain him with. He'd been out with Jane, and hadn't come home till two in the morning.

He stopped what he was doing to laugh, remembering her with that clock in her hand, raising it high above her head and swearing she would *brain* him with it. She'd picked up the clock because it had been the nearest thing to hand, but now the picture in Archie's memory made him think she was blaming him for the passing of time itself.

'*Ma, what time is it?*'

His mother hurried into the kitchen and began to bang things around on the cooker.

'There's a clock there, isn't there,' said his mother.

'Is it slow or fast?'

'It's right as far as I know.'

'It's always wrong,' said Archie. He fitted the first foot-sized piece of cardboard into his shoe, then picked up the second piece and started trimming it with the scissors.

'Ah'm gonnae miss this bus,' said Archie.

'Ye will if ye dinnae hurry,' said his mother. 'Where is it ye're goin anyway my lad?'

'Nowhere,' said Archie. 'Just out.'

135

'Well mind and watch yersel,' said his mother, 'and don't be late.'

'Aye ma,' said Archie in a bored voice. He concentrated on fitting the second piece of cardboard into the shoe.

'What a mess in here,' said his mother, as she stepped between the foot-shaped pieces of cardboard on the floor. She poured hot water from the kettle over the dirty dishes in the sink and went on: 'Reminds me of the time we went ballroom dancing, me and yer faither.'

'Before ma time,' said Archie. He struggled to fit the third piece into his other shoe, then took it out and trimmed it with the scissors. 'Ma, Ah need a new pair of shoes!'

'There's a perfectly good pair in the hall,' said his mother. 'He'd only worn them twice before he died.'

'A cannae wear *them*,' said Archie, 'Ah need a *new* pair!'

'We'll just have tae see,' said his mother. She laid the cups to drain on the steel draining board.

Archie stood up and stamped his feet on the kitchen floor. He pulled on his jacket.

'Would ye look at this mess,' said his mother, picking up a few pieces of cardboard and the bag with the cornflakes in it.

'Ah'll have tae run for that bus,' said Archie. Out in the hall and with a hand on the front door, he heard her calling:

'You mind and watch yersel now, and don't be late!'

He shaded his eyes with a hand because of the sun coming through the window. He looked at the way her arm curved at the wrist when she poured the water. He'd never been alone with her in the house like this before. There had always been her mother, or her sister, or her big brother in another room. Usually she took him into the front room, the one the family never used. He wasn't used to being with her in the kitchen like this, and that was making it harder to tell her.

He sat and watched her face as she chattered and made tea and smiled at him, as if tonight was like any other night. Was she beautiful? He couldn't tell, her face kept moving. All he could tell was that her skin looked dark against the light from the window, dark but sort of glowing, and when she looked at him her eyes were very alive. The other thing he could tell was that he would never sit here and watch her like this again as she moved around the room talking and smiling, because even if he did it would be different. She was changing into a different person all the time, and if she was beautiful it was all to do with this changing thing. She was smiling at him a lot, and that was making it harder.

He looked out of the window and tried to concentrate on a little cloud above the rooftops. It didn't seem to be going anywhere or doing anything. It was that kind of evening, as if time wasn't passing.

'You take sugar?' she said, and she laughed because she'd never made tea for him in her house like this before and it was ridiculous.

'Two,' said Archie, then he laughed too because he had never had tea in her house like this before and it was ridiculous. It was all a bit like they were married, and that was making it harder.

'My mum used to make tea for my dad, before he died,' said Archie. He liked saying things to her which were dead obvious as if they were dead interesting.

'It would be strange if she did after,' she said, laughing loudly.

'She does sometimes,' said Archie, 'sometimes she pours out an extra cup.'

'Really?'

He liked making her laugh like that, then saying something that made the laugh change into really. And he wanted to kiss her because she was interested in the cup laid out for the dead, and because of the way her eyebrows went when she said really. But kissing her would only make things harder.

She came over to him and handed him a cup of tea. He put it on the floor beside his foot, then felt uncomfortable because of the shoes. It was a nice kitchen, nicer than in his house – it even had chairs a bit like armchairs, as well as the ones round the table – and every so often he remembered about the shoes. The big holes in the soles, the heels worn down almost to the uppers.

The cardboard insoles he'd put in before leaving the house had worn through already, and now he could feel new holes – holes in the holes. The last time he'd taken her out – to the pictures to see a D. H. Lawrence film – she'd noticed the shoes. He'd turned from the ticket-booth and seen her looking down at his worn heels, then she'd looked up at him and tried to hide it, but he'd seen the pity in her eyes. He'd felt angry about the pity, and hadn't started kissing her till half-way through the film. They'd gone on kissing for most of the second half, and he'd got his hand up inside her blouse, then down inside her jeans. She'd told him she loved him, but wanted to see how it ended.

Archie stared at the shoes: the heels were worn down even more now. He looked out of the window: the cloud had moved. He looked at her face: changing. Soon her mother would be back from work. He would have to tell her soon.

She curled up in a chair opposite him and eyed him and licked at her tea.

'You look like a cat when you do that,' said Archie.

'Do what?' she said. She licked at the tea again and grinned.

'That,' said Archie.

She yawned and stretched out an arm. 'Did you go to your night-class last night?'

'Yeah.'

'What was it like?'

'Great. The teacher says I'll get an "A".'

'Then you'll go to Art College. D'you think you'll be a famous artist?'

Archie thought for a moment.

'Probably,' he said.

He was just about to cross his legs the way he had seen a famous artist doing it on TV, with one ankle resting on the other knee, when he remembered about the shoes.

'I wouldn't talk to you if you were a famous artist,' she said. She came over to him and sat on the floor in front of him, leaning her elbows on his knees. He drew his feet as far under the chair as they would go. 'I wouldn't even come to the phone if it was you.' Her eyes had that look in them that said *so there*.

'How come?' said Archie, although he knew she wasn't really serious. They were never really serious when they talked about anything, they just talked and let the words take them somewhere.

'I'd chuck you,' she said.

'What for?' said Archie, playing along. But he knew that all this would only make it harder.

'I'd be too embarrassed. It would be like going out with *Eamonn Andrews*.' She laughed loudly about this, but stopped half-way when Archie didn't join in. And he knew that he would be laughing too if not for the shoes and the pity.

'But you'd say hello to me in the street!' said Archie, as if he was really serious.

'Well, I suppose I'd say hello in the *street*!' She laughed again, but stopped this time as soon as she'd started. 'What's wrong with you?' she said, frowning. She pulled away from him and frowned at him as if she were his mother. And he wanted to kiss her again because she was trying to frown and she didn't have the kind of face which could frown really. He said nothing, but leaned forward and stared at his cup of tea. She tugged at his sleeve. 'Hey, what's the matter with you tonight?'

'Nothing.'

'There is. What's wrong? You're not here.'

'How d'you mean?'

'You're not *here*,' she repeated, tugging at both his sleeves and trying to pull him into here. When that failed, she sat back and looked at him with narrowed eyes. She was good at narrowed eyes. It was one of the things Archie liked about her, all the crazy things she could do with her face. 'Look,' she said, in the tones of an offended auntie, 'ye havnae even *touched* yer tea!'

Archie looked at the undrunk cup of tea at his foot and suddenly felt like laughing out loud because it was ridiculous. Suddenly everything was ridiculous: this being in the kitchen together as if they were married; his mother telling him to 'mind and watch yersel' before he'd come out; the extra cup poured out for the dead; her saying it would be like going out with

Eamonn Andrews. Everything made him want to laugh, everything was ridiculous. Everything except the shoes and the pity.
He concentrated on the holes in his soles as a way of stifling the
laughter. He waited for a minute, then he said it: 'I want to
finish it.'

He'd wondered how it would sound when he said it. Now
he'd said it, and he knew how it sounded. There was no beauty
in it, and no pity. It sounded ordinary and ridiculous. He didn't
look up, but heard her gasp.

'Why?'

When he did look up, he saw the first tear dripping from her
eyelashes. She leaned forwards to put her arms round his neck,
and the tear fell into his cup of tea. Then he could feel her mouth
up against his ear and she was asking him why again. When she
pulled away, her cheeks were wet with the tears.

'Are you fed up with me?'

'It's not that.'

'Why then?'

'It's just . . . time to finish it, that's all.'

'Time?'

She looked at the clock on the wall, as if the real explanation
might be found there. Archie looked at it. It was the kind of
clock his mother would have liked to possess.

'Who's that?' said Archie, as they heard the front door
opening and someone coming into the hall.

It was getting dark when Archie opened the door of the
Boulevard Café in the High Street. He went in and saw Charlie
there, sitting at the corner table they always sat at.

'Well,' said Charlie, 'how d'it go?'

Archie said nothing, but hung his head. He waited for the
waitress to come, then ordered a tea.

'Did ye tell her?' said Charlie. Archie nodded and stared at
the table. Charlie gave a long, low whistle. He was good at long,
low whistles. 'Did ye pick the right time, the right moment?'

'There isn't a right time for it,' said Archie.

'Right enough,' said Charlie, 'But tell me what happened,

THE SHOES

eh? What did ye say? How did she take it?'

Archie shook his head and stared at the table.

'Okay,' said Charlie, 'tell me later.'

Both sat staring at the table until Charlie thought of something else to talk about.

'Hey,' he said, 'what d'ye thinka these then?' He raised one leg above the level of the table, then pointed the toe of his shoe first one way, then another. He swung round in the seat and raised the other leg, so that both shoes were visible. 'Just got them the day. What d'ye thinka them? They're magic, eh?'

'Magic,' said Archie, without looking at the shoes. Then he did glance at them. They had cuban heels and chiselled toes and elasticated gussets down the insides, they were black and shiny and new, and he saw that they really were magic.

ANDY'S TRIAL

William Miller

Andy walked along, looking at the row of cards in the Job Centre. Looking, but not seeing.

Fifteen months, he was thinking, since he had left school. Only one job, and that had lasted a mere four days. He had learned that he did not have a natural talent for driving a fork-lift truck. On the other hand, the foreman, who had seemed to be quite a reasonable man, might have been more understanding. After all, it had been a fairly small wall . . .

The only thing, he reflected, that he had become skilled at over the past year and a quarter was lying on his back in bed, staring at the ceiling.

Andy's eyes slowly began to focus. 'Part time dishwasher – £30 p.w.; Steeplejack; Time-served welder, £120 plus bonus.' Then his heart leapt. He couldn't believe it! 'Defence Lawyer for GBH case – no previous experience required.'

He glanced quickly around. There were only two others looking at the vacancies. Neither seemed likely competition, but he decided to move quickly. He walked over to the desk.

'Lawyer's joab!' He said to the man behind the counter, in a voice that he hoped sounded confident. The clerk looked at him dispassionately.

'Ye're gey young,' he said. 'Ah widney think ye could handle it.'

Andy screwed his face into what he fancied was a superior expression.

'Oh, ah'll handle it aw right,' he replied. 'Ah've seen aw the auld Perry Mason shows oan the telly.'

'Uh-huh!' retorted the clerk. 'Mebbe so. But fur this joab

ye've goat tae be able tae lie oan yer back an' stare at the
ceilin'!' A smug expression accompanied the statement.

Andy smiled inwardly.

'He thinks he's goat me wi that wan.' Aloud, he said airily,
'Nae bother mister. Ah've been practisin fur a year. Ah'm an
expert. Ah can dae it staunin' oan mah heid. D'ye want me tae
show ye?'

'Naw naw. Ah'll take yer word fur it.' The clerk was looking
at him now with some respect.

'Huv ye goat 'O' levels in Woodwork an' Geography?' he
asked.

'Aye,' replied Andy. ' 'N metal work an' aw.'

'Oh here, that's great,' exclaimed the clerk. 'Ah think ye're in
wae a chance. Kin ye talk posh?'

'Nae bother,' Andy responded, trying hard. 'Nae bother at
all.'

'There's only wan ither wee proablem,' the clerk went on.
'Ye're a bit scruffy lookin'.' He paused for a moment. 'Tell ye
whit,' he continued, 'here's a social security cheque fur a fancy
suit.' He produced a slip of paper from the desk.

'D'ye know wherr the high court is?'

Andy nodded. Another piece of paper appeared.

'Jist gie this tae the man at the door, an ye'll get in.'

Andy, resplendent in a pin-stripe suit and carrying a briefcase
which contained nothing more legal than a couple of cheese
sandwiches, arrived at the door of Courtroom Six.

'Counsel fur the defence,' he said to the man who appeared to
be guarding the entrance.

'You the fella frae the Joab Centre?' asked the man.

'Aye,' replied Andy. 'how did ye know?'

'The label,' said the man, opening the door.

Andy looked down and saw that there was indeed a label
stuck to the top pocket of his jacket which said 'YTS Defence
Counsel'. He hurriedly removed it and went through the
door.

The courtroom was crowded but Andy saw an empty seat

behind a table in the well of the court. He made his way towards it, acknowledging as he went, by a slight inclination of his head, the deference shown to him by the common people in the public gallery.

He had only just sat down behind a pile of important-looking papers, when a voice shouted 'Wid yis aw staun up!'

Andy obeyed the injunction. The judge, an old man in a Santa Claus cloak and a grubby looking wig, appeared through a door and ascended to a raised position behind a bench overlooking the whole courtroom.

The judge sat down and said to no one in particular, 'Ah'm fair puffed. They stairs get worse every day.' Then he produced a hammer with which he banged the bench several times in evident satisfaction.

'Who's persecutin'?' he called in a high pitched voice.

'I am!' A thin-faced man with a long nose and dark hair carefully plastered over a bald patch rose to his feet.

'Right then,' said the judge, waving a dismissive hand, 'who's the Defender?'

Andy stood up proudly. 'Me, yer honour,' he called.

The judge peered at him over a pair of spectacles that were perched on the end of his nose.

'Oh here, ah fair like yer suit son,' he said.

The thin-faced man sprang to his feet. 'Objection!' he shouted. 'You never said you liked *my* suit.'

'Shut up!' said the judge, fairly politely. 'Objection over-ruled. Yours doesny fit ye right.'

The thin-faced man frowned and sat down, muttering to himself. For a moment nothing seemed to be happening, so Andy stood up, put his thumbs into his waistcoat pockets and began to speak.

'Ladies an' Gentlemen o' the jury,' he began. 'Ah wid jist like fur tae say . . .'

The judge banged his hammer again. 'It's no your turn yet, son,' he said.

Andy bowed his head. 'Sorry, yer honour. Ah huvny done much lawyerin' afore.'

'Don't apologize. Don't apologize.' The judge pointed his hammer. 'Mr Weasel gets the first shot.'

The thin-faced man stood up with a condescending smile on his face. 'Ai wid like to call the injured pairty of the first pairt,' he said loudly.

Andy sensed trouble. His adversary had a posher voice than the judge.

'The injured pairty!' came a disembodied voice, the call being repeated several times, each fainter than the last.

'Jist like the films,' thought Andy.

Eventually the injured party appeared in the witness box. He was six feet tall, heavily built, had large ears and a flattened nose.

'He isny hauf the injured pairty!' burst out Andy.

Once again, the judge brought down his hammer on the bench. 'Ye canny say things like that son,' he pronounced. 'No here, onywey.'

The thin faced man addressed the man in the witness box. 'Will you please tell us your name?'

Andy couldn't believe it. 'Ye're no much o' a lawyer if ye doant know his name by this time! He's your client.'

'D' *you* know his name?' asked Mr Weasel.

'Naw – but –'

'Well, don't get smart wi' me.'

'Gentlemen! Gentlemen!' called the judge. Then, addressing Andy, 'Ah know ye're jist startin' son, but did they no gie ye a book o' rules at the Joab Centre?'

Andy shook his head.

'Gie him a book Fred,' said the judge.

A small blue pamphlet appeared on Andy's table. He opened it and read: '1. Speak proper; 2. Wait your turn; 3. No rude gestures; 4. The judge is quite a nice old man.'

The judge was smiling and nodding towards Andy. 'Okay? Right, get oan wey it.'

Mr Weasel again spoke to the man in the witness box: 'Wid you tell the court whit yer name is?'

'Cornelius Sandpaper.'

'Please, yer honour,' called Andy, 'Ah think that's a sody name.'

'A whit?' asked the judge.

'A sody name – he's makin' it up.'

The judge looked down at some papers. 'Naw,' he pronounced. 'It's right enough. That's his name.'

'Goad Almighty,' said Andy.

The judge frowned and signalled to Andy to turn over a page of his pamphlet: '5. No swearing.'

'Sorry yer honour.'

Mr Weasel, who had sat down during this interchange, rose once more to his feet. 'Mr Sandpaper, will you tell the court in your own words whit happened at the scene o' the crime.'

Andy jumped to his feet. 'Objection!' he cried. 'We huvny asser – asser – made oot – that a crime wis committed!'

The judge smiled benignly. 'Oh, helluva good son. Ye're learnin' real fast.'

Andy felt himself blushing. 'Thanks very much,' he answered, and sat down quickly.

His adversary scowled. 'Wid you tell the court?' he continued, 'exactly what happened?'

The injured party cleared his throat. 'Ah wis walkin' through this supermarket . . .'

Again Andy rose to his feet. 'Whit supermarket?'

'Aw! Wait a *minit*!' said Mr Weasel to the judge. 'It's *my* turn. Ye'll have tae make him shut up, Uncle George.'

The judge's face turned purple. 'Don't call me Uncle George, will ye no Alistair. Ah see ah'll hae tae huv anither word wae yer mother.'

Mr Weasel looked suitably abashed as the judge turned to Andy.

'Son,' he said, 'ye'll need tae keep yer mooth shut till it's your turn. Sit doon, will ye!'

Andy sat.

'Please continue, Mr Sandpaper,' asked Mr Weasel.

'Ah wis jist walkin' through this supermarket, lookin' fur six cans o' export,' said the injured party, 'when this auld biddy hit me oan the heid wae a tin o' baked beans.'

'Whit auld biddy?' prompted Mr Weasel. 'Can ye point her out?'

The injured party indicated a white-haired elderly woman who was standing between two policewomen.

'Aw, definitely objection this time!' Andy shouted, positively leaping to his feet. 'That's mah Granny!'

The judge brought down his hammer in front of him so hard that it almost flew from his grasp.

'Good point, son,' he said. 'Whit huv ye goat tae say tae that Alist – eh, Mr Weasel?'

The person so addressed stood up straight and looked down his nose at Andy. 'It's no German tae the issue,' he retorted.

The judge looked sadly at Andy. 'Ah'm afraid he's goat ye there, son!'

Andy sank back into his chair. Weasel-face smirked and continued: 'Kin you tell me what the motive was fur this crime?'

Mr Sandpaper considered the question for some moments, then replied, 'Malice aforethought.'

Again, Andy couldn't contain himself. 'Well, if it wis Alice Whityecaller, whits mah Granny daein the dock? Her name's Margaret.'

The judge shook his head. 'Son,' he said, 'ye'll need tae get yersel' sorted oot inside that fancy suit o' yours, or ye'll get yer books.'

Andy subsided, feeling confused. 'It's no fair,' he muttered, 'her name's Margaret.'

'Mah learned friend is labouring under a misapprehension,' said Mr Weasel. 'Mah learned friend is just showing aff-off his poor education.'

The judge glared. 'Doan't get personal, Alistair. Onywey, ye canny say that. The boy's goat 'O' Levels in Woodwork and Geography. Huv ye ony mair questions tae ask the witness?'

'No, your Honour. Ye can ask mah learned friend tae cross-examine.'

'Ony time ye bloody want,' retorted Andy.

'Language, Language!' called the judge, holding up a copy of the pamphlet. 'Remember where yis are.'

Andy stood up and, staring hard at the injured party, asked in an offhand manner, 'Whit size o' tin wis it?'

Mr Sandpaper looked baffled. Mr Weasel jumped to his feet with an objection.

'What difference dis it make what size it wis?'

Andy gave him a scornful glance. 'Ye widnae be askin' that if it wis you that goat hit.'

There was laughter in court and the judge said, 'Good fur you, son.'

'Ah'll ask ye again. Whit size o' tin wis it?'

'Ah'm no sure,' replied the injured party. 'Ah think it wis wan o' these meteoric wans.'

'Ye mean metric.'

'Aye, ah suppose so. But it wis gawin' at a helluva speed.'

Andy gave him a withering stare. 'Did ye actually see mah Granny – ah mean, the accused, fling it?'

'No in so many words.'

'Well then,' continued Andy, feeling very much in control of the situation, 'Well then, ah pit it tae ye that the hale thing is a fabrication o' tissues!'

'Good fur you, wee Andy!' shouted his grandmother.

The judge looked over his specs. 'Mah dear wumman,' he said patiently, 'will ye kindly shut yer geggie? This is a court o' law, and accused persons who speak oot o' turn get the heavies pit ontae them.'

The old lady bowed her head. 'Sorry, yer highness.'

Andy was a bit peeved at this. 'Ye shouldny speak tae mah Granny like that,' he said sharply.

'Now son,' retorted the judge, 'don't let that fancy suit go tae yer heid. Jist get oan wae it.'

Andy again put his thumbs in his waistcoat pockets. 'Now, then, mah good man,' he began. He liked the phrase so much that he repeated it. 'Now, then, mah good man, whit makes ye think it wis mah Granny that hit ye wae the metric beans?'

The injured party drew himself to his full height and glared at Andy. 'It couldny huv been onybuddy else.'

'How no?'

'Well – there wis jist the baith o' us there. Ah wis jist – ah wis jist . . .'

As he hesitated there was a sudden stir from the dock and Andy's Granny shrieked, 'He wis efter mah boady!!'

There was consternation in court, and the judge went absolutely daft with his hammer. 'Silence in court!' he shouted several times. Then, when some semblance of order was resumed, he turned towards the accused person and said conversationally, 'This is jist a common assault case. It isny Burke an' Hare.'

The comment took a moment or two to sink in. Then, 'Ye cheeky auld bugger!' shouted Andy's Granny.

There was a startled silence. The judge shook his head sadly. 'Listen, dearie,' he said. 'Ah kin say whit ah like tae you. Ah'm the judge. But you canny say whit ye like tae me. If you call me names like that again, ah'll huv ye fur bein' contemptible.'

The accused covered her mouth with her hand and stuck her tongue out, but said no more.

'Uncle George!' shouted Weasel-face. 'She stuck her tongue out.'

'Don't be a clipe, Alistair,' retorted the judge, firmly.

'Yer Honour,' interjected Andy, 'ye'll huv tae forgive the accused. She's usually at the Bingo at this time.'

'I understand, son.' The judge smiled. 'Carry on.'

Andy turned again towards the injured party. 'Ah think ye better explain yersel, Pie-face.'

Mr Weasel, who was becoming extremely fed up at the judge's attitude towards Andy, rose to his feet. 'Aw, come on, Uncle George. Ye canny let him say things like that tae mah client. It's his Granny that's on trial.'

'Listen, Alistair,' said the judge, through clenched teeth, 'Ah'm no gonny tell ye again. Forget the Uncle George stuff, or ah'll dae somethin' nasty tae yer credentials!' He turned to

Andy. 'Ah tell't his mother he wid never make a lawyer, but, ach, naebuddy ever listens tae me.'

'Ah dae yer honour,' said Andy.

'Aye. So ye dae, son,' replied the judge.

'Crawler!' shouted Weasel-face.

'Jist ignore him,' the judge said. 'Carry on son, yer dain' marvellous.'

Andy, swelling with pride, returned to the attack with renewed vigour.

'Ah pit it tae ye that oan the 9th April, 1984 ye wir in a supermarket, tryin' tae interfere wae mah Granny's boady, an' she defended hersel wae a tin o' Heinz's beans.'

'Listen, Mister,' replied the injured party, 'Ah widny interfere wae yer Granny if she wis about tae step under a bus! Ah wis jist reachin' ower fur a six pack, when mah airm must a' brushed against her chist.'

'Aha!' cried Andy, 'so ye admit it!'

'Ah admit nothin'. Maybe it wis her chist that brushed against mah airm. Whitiver wey ye pit it, it wisny much o' a thrill. Then, the next thing ah know, ah wis unconscientious.'

'Serve ye bliddy well right!' Andy retorted.

'Language, language,' admonished the judge for the second time. 'Onyway, ah'm gettin' a sair heid wi' aw this evidence. Ah think we'll chuck it an' get oan wae the closin' speeches. You kin huv the first go, Alist – Mr Weasel.'

'Ladies and Gentlemen o' the jury,' began the prosecuting counsel, 'youse have all heard the evidence that my client was the object o' an unprovoked attack delivered by the enemy of society ye see in the dock there. Don't be deceived by her white hair and bad feet. My client, Mr Cornelius Sandpaper, who is a kind and gentle man –'

At this point the injured party went all coy and grinned nervously, showing a row of yellow, uneven teeth.

'My client,' went on Mr Weasel, 'was struck down in the flooer o' his youth by a septuagenerian hooligan –'

'Ah'm only sixty-four,' shouted Andy's Granny.

Mr Weasel ignored the interruption. 'Mr Sandpaper,' he

continued, 'wis walloped for no good reason. Mugged, in a supermarket, in broad daylight, by the defending coonsel's Granny. Ladies and Gentlemen, youse have a duty to our fair land o' Scotland, to prevent it degenerating doon the drain intae anarchy . . .'

'That's in Italy,' thought Andy, but he stayed silent.

'. . . So I ask youse, Ladies and Gentlemen, to deliver the maximum sentence possible for this Heinz's crime.' He spread his arms wide in an appealing gesture. 'In the name of justice,' he concluded, 'I rest my case!'

The judge was smiling broadly. 'That wis quite good, Alistair,' he said. 'Ye're improvin'.'

He turned towards Andy. 'Your turn noo. On ye go.'

'Friends,' began Andy, 'and fellow members o' the workin' class . . .'

Out of the corner of his eye he saw the judge shaking his head disapprovingly. He realized that he had made a mistake. Several members of the jury obviously didn't think that they were working class. He couldn't understand that, since he was enjoying the novelty, but he started again.

'Friends,' he said, 'youse are all very intelligent people.' That was obviously better. Several of the jury were smiling self-consciously. 'Youse will therefore unnerstaun,' he went on, 'that mah – that the accused grey-haired old person wis in the supermarket, desperately trying fur tae make her pension go far enough tae cover luxuries, like food. Tryin' tae stretch her widow's mite –'

'Don't tell lies, Andy,' said his grandmother sharply. 'Ye know yer Grandad's still alive. Well – jist aboot.'

'Sorry Granny, Ah'm dain' mah best.'

'Aye, so ye are, Son. Ye're a good boy.'

Andy determined to do even better. 'This poor auld wumman, who hus been a Granny tae me aw mah life. –' (here he thought he saw tears steal into the eyes of several of the jury so he repeated himself) 'This poor auld wumman –'

'Aw, come on Andy, ahm no *that* auld!'

'– who hus been a Granny tae me aw mah days, wis wonder-in' whit she could buy wae her last forty pence, and hud jist picked up a tin o' beans, when this big ugly guy –'

'Ye're nae ile paintin yersel',' interjected the injured party.

Andy ignored the interruption. '. . . When this big ugly guy went fur her.'

'Went fur her whit?' asked the judge.

'Jist – went fur her. Anyway, she turned roon an saw this – this big gorilla tryin' tae take unfair advantage o' her. So she did whit onybuddy's Granny wid dae. She belted him wan oan the bean wae the beans.' He smiled towards the jury, enjoying his joke, but saw that they were not returning his smile.

'Don't tell me they've nae sense o' humour,' he thought, and continued, 'So ah pit it tae yis that the persecution's case is a load o' tripe, thrown up as a smokescreen fur tae hide the identity o' the real criminal, who is staunin' there, looking as if butter widny melt in his boots. Ah ask yis tae throw this case oot the windae!'

And on that emphatic note he sat down, feeling well pleased with himself.

He got a round of applause from his Granny.

'Is that it?' asked the judge.

Andy nodded.

The judge hitched his gown around his neck. 'Noo it's mah turn,' he said. 'Ahm the heid bummer in here, so ah get tae hae the last word. Ah huv tae sum up the evidence as they say.' He looked at the jury. 'If it gets ower technical fur ye, ye're no allowed tae ask questions, so pey attention!' He took a deep breath. 'Oan the wan hand he' – pointing to his nephew – 'says the auld wumman done it.'

At this there was a muffled sound from the accused person.

'Oan the ither hand he' – indicating Andy – 'says she acted in self-defence. So, Ladies an' Gentleman, it's up tae youse tae make up yer minds – and don't take aw day, fur ah'm needin' mah dinner!'

The jury filed out, and a low murmur of voices filled the courtroom as everyone began to debate what the verdict might be. Andy, although sure he had done enough to get his Granny off, was nervous. He looked around the court. Mr Weasel was surreptitiously picking his nose. The judge had got out a needle and thread and was apparently darning a hole in his robes.

Someone in the public gallery started singing 'Happy Days are Here Again', but desisted when struck across the head by an usher wielding a rolled-up copy of the *Daily Mirror*.

After a seemingly endless wait, the jury returned, and when asked what the verdict was the foreman replied: 'We find the accused white-haired auld person guilty, notwithstanding her sair feet; but wid ask that the sentence considers the effect o' inflation on the price o' beans.'

Andy's heart sank, but he leapt to his feet. 'Objection! Yer Honour!'

The judge sighed. 'Ye canny object tae the verdict, son. It wis aw done fair. Onywey,' he smiled, 'ye goat a fancy new suit oot o' it, didn't ye?'

'But whit aboot mah Granny?'

The judge sighed again. 'Ach, this is the bit ah hate.' He reached under his desk and produced a black cap which he placed on his head.

'Ah sentence the prisoner tae be incarcerated in the nearest jile and fur tae dae sixty years slightly hard labour.'

'But, yer honour,' shouted Andy, 'she's sixty-five now. She'll never make it!'

'Well, she'll just hae tae dae the best she can. We'll no take it too personal if she kicks the bucket afore her time's oot.'

'Andy!' shouted his Granny across the courtroom as she was being led away. 'Ye'll need tae dae somethin'! Ah'm supposed tae be gettin' yer Grandad's dinner ready.'

Andy, who for some reason had begun to think he was dreaming, sighed deeply. He supposed that now it would be up to him to get his Grandad's dinner prepared. He hoped he didn't burn the mince. His Grandad could be real crabbit, sometimes . . .

JANE'S RAT

Chris Retzler

I guess quite a few of my friends are single parents – mostly women of course, but the occasional man too. And I find out about their kids in the normal course of things – I meet them on the bus, or being taken to school. It's an ordinary enough fact of life, but with some people I find out just a little later than I'd expect.

Robbie had invited me for dinner, and to make it simpler for me to get there, we met up in town after work and caught the bus out together. We had to walk about quarter of a mile at the other end: her place was at the end of a lane of cottages, set a little apart from the rest. It was a summer evening, and I suddenly wished I lived in the country too – it smelled so different, so calm.

On her doorstep she fumbled with her key while I admired the highlights in her hair. She turned to me – we both jumped at finding our faces suddenly so close together – and said breathlessly, 'Oh – my daughter Jane has a rat.' Perhaps she thought the two pieces of information would be twice as easy to accept.

She pushed open the door, we went in. Jane was at the table in the living room. Serious, seven years old. She was turning the handle of a little musical box that was playing 'Rudolph the Red-nosed Reindeer', and the rat was dancing on the table. Robbie looked vexed. 'Jane dear, you mustn't encourage him to dance on the table.' To me, it didn't look like the kind of rat that would need any encouragement to dance on the table or anywhere else for that matter. It looked the kind of rat that, given the right mood music, would be happy to undertake the most ostentatious performances. I decided that the tango

would suit it well, all those theatrical head turns and melod-
ramatic glances.

The pair of them had reached the sad bit about never letting
poor Rudolph join in any reindeer games. Jane was quavering
the words, and the rat was sniffling.

'It's just that, well, rats are often not terribly clean, dear.'

'I just bathed him,' said Jane indignantly. 'And I washed his
feet special.' The rat looked hurt. Robbie sighed and went to get
supper.

'Only two hundred more days till Christmas!' I said heartily.
Jane gave me a withering glance. 'Are you silly?' she asked, in a
tone that made me want to make a clean breast of it there and
then.

Robbie came back with a pot of stew and three large soup
plates held underneath it. She served it out. Jane told us about
her day at school. They had a new teacher, with a stutter – she
took it off rather well. My theory is that on leaving teacher
training college, if you don't have some quirk or other already,
you're provided with one, so the kids have something to laugh
at and don't feel intimidated.

The rat meanwhile was playing with the remote control for
the telly. After a stern glance from Robbie, it had turned the
sound down, but was playing with the colour balance. Anna
Ford was now the colour that Reggie Bosanquet always used to
be. The rat was kicking its little legs up and falling back on the
sofa in silent laughter. 'He's my rat,' explained Jane.

I don't know what I'd expected of the evening – something
along the lines of a candlelit supper I suppose. I probably do
mean that euphemistically, too. This was very different, but in
its own way more intimate. A glimpse of someone's domestic
life. And seeing children at home, one to one, rather than in
terrifying alien hordes streaming out of schools, is really special. It lets me feel connected to my own childhood.

Robbie took Jane to bed, saying she'd read her a story. I read
a magazine. When she came back she said simply, 'We should
let her settle down.' So I was able to reach across and kiss her as
though it were the hundredth time, and not the first.

Later we undressed in her room, together in the dark. She went and opened the window to the night, then came back to me, all curve and shadow. Like both of us coming home.

It used to freak me a bit, this habit of hers of opening the window each time. It had a symbolism – as though to let out all the sounds that should by rights be free – quite the opposite of what my puritan, private streak demanded. But then again, when I'm just watching TV I close all the doors and windows too, so maybe I just have a morbid fear of draughts.

I spent more and more time out at the cottage, sharing in the housework and gardening. The rat was – well, if not actually suspicious of me, at least very cautious. It would glance at me covertly as it sat playing with the speak-and-spell, which it was rather good at. I used to take along chocolate to try and bribe my way into favour. It worked fine with Jane. She would hold the bar in one hand, wipe her chocolate-covered mouth with the other and come and jump in my crotch. This is the way kids express their affection and ease with adults, I've noticed. But the rat would eat the one square that Jane had given it ('I don't want him to be sick') quietly and seriously, saving the nuts till last, looking at me quizzically, trying to guess my motives. Made me feel so guilty.

Afterwards it would climb onto the table and practise its dancing. Robbie had given in by this time, and in fact had made it a tiny pair of lederhosen with proper Bavarian braces. The rat loved them, and would schuhplattel gaily. It had taught itself to yodel too, so we would have these very entertaining evenings that we could feel completely guilt-free about because they were so cultural.

It was strange that as things improved between Jane and her little friend and me, my relationship with Robbie was – oh I don't know, cooling, changing anyhow. We still needed very much to hold each other, but these nights the window stayed closed. In the morning Jane would squeeze in between us, cuddling either one indiscriminately, her body angular in the brushed cotton nightie. The rat never came, which I was glad of. It was just a little too sudden, its feet were too tiny, too pink.

I asked Robbie how long rats lived. She paled. 'Oh don't. I know it'll happen someday, I just hope she's a lot older.' In fact the rat showed not the least sign of slowing down. It seemed to have initiative and drive that would be unusual in a human, never mind a rodent. It had progressed from the speak-and-spell, via attentiveness to Jane's bedtime stories, to reading picture books on its own. I found it impressive – but sinister.

Jane told us at supper that she and the rat were going on a secret expedition to run away to ballet school. It was obvious who'd put her up to it. She usually told us about the secret picnics they were going on; it made it easier to get interesting food, and anyway, what's the fun of a secret if you can't tell anyone? On this occasion though I should have paid more attention.

Over the past week or so I'd had less and less attention to give. There seemed less point in coming out here, the bus rides seemed longer – especially as the nights drew in.

A few days later we were watching some modern dance on the telly. Jane and the rat sat transfixed for the whole hour. I liked it too, it was good, not too abstract. When it finished Robbie said to me, 'Chris, what do you think of dance classes for Jane?' And I laughed before I could stop myself: just the contrast of that gawky little body with the grace of the dancers we'd just seen. And I saw Jane flinch and that hurt like hell. I tried to repair the damage, saying yes, I thought it would be lovely, really good for her to do – maybe, I added lamely, she could get as good as the rat. But I could feel the whole room filled with wrongness.

In the kitchen, making tea, alone with Robbie, I said awkwardly, 'Look, I know I shouldn't have laughed. But let's face it, the girl's not exactly poetry in motion is she?' Robbie didn't look at me. 'It's not her talents which are at issue. It's her feelings. Our feelings. If I were single, Chris, I could flirt with you and let you flirt with me. But don't play with her affections, I can't bear it, it's too important. We're a package deal, my family and I, that's the reality. You've got to face that reality.'

She shouldn't have said that. She was right, but she

shouldn't have said it. In that instant I saw with too painful clarity the worry lines around her eyes, the need for truth and directness in her eyes, the rounding of her shoulders and the tension in her neck. All from cares I'd done too little to alleviate. I walked out of the kitchen, not knowing whether I wanted to walk out of the house altogether. At the living room door I stopped. Inside, at the table, was a girl. Seven years old, neither pretty nor plain. Her right cheek was resting on her left hand, flat on the table. Her right hand was stretched out across the table and stroking a pet rat.

CAFÉ DES
DEUX SOURIS

Brenda Shaw

It was a hellish summer. Blazing hot. Just blazing. The temperature hung between 80 and 90 for three months and the flies were everywhere. We had to keep the windows open for air and the screens were full of holes. Flies and mice. Almost more mice than flies.

I love mice, but they turd on everything – all over the floor, in the plant pots, on the kitchen table, in the cupboards, in the orange crate where we kept the tinned stuff. Always mouse turds.

They were cute, those mice. They played and hopped from plant pot to plant pot and even climbed up the Swiss cheese plant and sat on the leaves munching the pieces of cracker we put out for them. But then they discovered the avocado plant's leaves were good to eat and started chewing them. Must have shinneyed right up the stalk to get to them. Nipped the tender little green tops right off.

I painted a mouse café on the skirting board around one of their holes and put a sign on it, 'Café Des Deux Souris' and painted umbrellas and chairs and 'Café', 'Tabac', 'Vin' signs.

But the mouse turds got worse and worse and I read a book about bubonic plague and I closed up the mouse holes with plaster of Paris. I knew it was going to upset Ken. He loved those mice. They seemed to soothe him when he was too nervous to work. He used to sit on the couch and read or write and watch them come out to nibble their crackers and play and hop among the plants. Called them the Furry-scurries, or the Furry-burry-hurry-scurries. We called each other names like that too: Purry-burry and Purry-snug and Cuddles.

Yes, I knew it would upset him that I'd filled in the holes, but I thought he'd understand why. But when he got home and saw what I'd done he went livid. 'What the Hell have you done, Babe?'

I told him about the plague.

'For Christ's sakes, do you believe every fucking thing you read? Unplug those holes!'

'But it's not just plague, it's worms and typhoid and salmonella, and they've crapped all through the cupboard and in the flour. I'm surprised the landlord hasn't put down poison . . .'

He went from livid to red in a second and came at me roaring, 'Are you trying to fuck up my whole life? Unplug those holes, you bitch, or I'll cream the hell out of you!'

I got down on my hands and knees beside the Café des Deux Souris and began tearing at the plaster of Paris with my fingernails. No good, it had set hard and all my nails broke off. 'It won't come out,' I gasped.

He roared in a way I'd never heard before and I got up and started to run. He was between me and the door to the corridor so I ran into the bedroom, with him snarling behind me. There was no way out but the window, three storeys up, and it was closed. No time to open it – and I was as afraid of going through broken glass as I was of Ken. I threw myself on the bed and covered my head with my arms to ward off the blow.

But Ken stopped at the bedroom door. I didn't even hear him breathe for a minute. Then he closed the door – with him outside – and said through it, 'For the love of God don't come out.' Then he began to sob.

He cried for a long time, then I heard him moving about. He went out of the living room and then came back again and I heard pounding and scraping. In a little while he said, 'You can come out now.' He was ghastly white and there were blue marks under his eyes, but they were no longer wild. There were chunks of plaster of Paris and dust around the entrance to the Café des Deux Souris where he had opened it up.

'Don't you ever do anything like that again,' he said.

'I won't,' I whispered. Then I went into the bathroom and was sick.

About a week later Ken was out at the library. It was late afternoon and I was lying on the couch reading. Suddenly I heard a rattle and commotion in the papers by the bed. Must be the mice playing. Then a mouse ran out very fast and got out into the middle of the floor and began to stagger around in a circle and drag one leg. Then he collapsed on his side and I thought Oh God, he's going to die – did I hurt him somehow? Step on those papers when he was hiding in them maybe? I hope he isn't dying, maybe he's just playing – but they don't play like that – he's kicking. Oh poor thing, poor thing! Now he's stopped kicking. I can't see very well from here. He must be dead.

It was a long time before I could make myself get up to look at him. I tried to read but I'd keep glancing up and seeing the little body lying there on the floor.

Finally I got up and looked. He was dead, with his eyes open and dull, and a pink puddle of liquid coming out his tail end. It wasn't blood, just pale pink liquid.

I didn't kill that mouse, I thought. I couldn't have. I wasn't near those papers for hours. The landlord must have put down poison. But Ken'll never believe it. This time he won't stop at the bedroom door. The library closes at five, he'll be home any minute. My feet have grown into the floor. I can't move. There's no escape. I can't run. I'll have to stay here and let him kill me!

The door below banged and I jumped a good foot off the floor. I grabbed my shoulder bag from the table and ran through the flat to the outer door. I met Ken on the stairs half way up.

'Oh Honey, I forgot to get eggs and milk when I went shopping. If I'm quick I can just get to the shop before it closes. I'll be back in a few minutes.'

'Okay, Babe,' he said, kissing my ear.

When I got outside I ran like hell around the corner of the building, over the back fence and up the alley to Kirkton Street, down Kirkton, through several derelict back lots and onto Terrance Avenue. There was a streetcar approaching the stop and I flagged it down.

'Where to, Miss?' asked the driver as I flung myself on board. I didn't know where the hell it was going.

'The end of the line,' I said.

MOANA

Jackson Webb

Time and again, the great tides poured through Manihiki. The long-legged terns wandered closer, the dozing reef gulls floated in. The weight and peace of the sea spread deeper, blue shadows and lights by the inlet house.

A girl poled her boat down the rising shallows. She tied it to a jetty in the mangroves across and disappeared with a step in the walls of pandanus. I welcomed the daily sight of her passing, as she grinned and nodded her shredded straw hat, the only event in the blurs of hours.

One afternoon, I went to meet her. The blue dragonflies were pinging along the banks and the myna birds screeched from the dimness of vines. There were voices in the shade of the bamboo landing, breathing and shell-clicks in the islets of flax: sounds I missed from my tin-roofed veranda. The wind touched the palms over Father John's church. The launch chugged out in the brassy lagoon. But in the trees across the inlet, evening had begun. The spirals of mosquitos started to sing. A sandpiper blinked from the edge of the leaves.

Her face and wide shoulders parted the reeds and she called a line of words at once. 'Yis, right it is! Quite a fine day!'

'The water comes in fast,' I said.

'Aye, fast-coming.' She smiled at me blankly.

Tom Wilkov had seen us from the company launch, winding through the reef pass with his knee on the tiller.

'Been across there, have you?' he grinned. 'Oh, well! Prime bit of land – I fancy it myself. Crew of boys could cut it back in a fortnight. That gives you the inlet for pineapple country.'

Cook Islands Company Store stood under a flame tree at the

163

end of the beach, sudden, open-fronted, with its bright shelves full and its slow-moving fan. Boat parts, cement sacks, sheets of scored tin – barbed wire, machettes, whisky, dog food: Cook-islandstore. People ran the words together, like Fatherjohn and *Cometwindsydney*, the rusty schooner broken over the reef.

Tom Wilkov owned most of the island now. Cashcredit. Tradeunderstandings. He had a diesel winch that roared like a buzz saw, yanking up oil drums and heaps of tan copra. He was also the butcher, the welder and bank. His workshop was in the shack at the side, a jumble of tools and oily machinery where he pounded and watched through the dank afternoons. Some said he was Scottish, some said Russian. He had come to the Cooks about thirty years ago, when Father John had brought people down from the hill, given them clothes and taken their dancing.

I saw her at the Sunday market, arm in arm with two laughing fat friends. She wore a green paru and a lei of gardenias. She stopped with her basket by the planks on the pier while the others rolled on through the melons and shouts. Her name was Moana. I said it again. How long would it be until next time?

The priest nudged between us with a fish in a paper, then came the policeman's exhausted pony, eating an orange and flicking his tail. Moana whispered something funny, poked me with her finger, even. I liked her loose bracelets and fall-apart hat. She let me see her as she stood beside me, fresh and sure, the surprise of her there.

I painted the boats on the violet lagoon. The fireflies skimmed through the listening nights. I'd been there four months and no work had happened. Tell me the use of making journeys.

I sketched the reef and the lapping jetty. I drew the nets in the clear green water. One morning, I saw a faraway ship, a pencil line with a curl of smoke, diving down in the distance again.

I couldn't account for the time before this. The year in New Zealand seemed nearer than now. Manihiki. Unapproachable place, mixed and defeated, not even my choice but a fought-through error.

Father John paid a call and warned me gently: 'Make no mistake. Example is help.'

He stood at my gate with his basin hat, always thinking of more to say. 'It is selfish to do otherwise. That is my conviction.'

Could you say what you thought to grim Father John, the same dark sight all the way down the path?

The trade winds lifted a far curve of thunderheads, higher and whiter, straight overhead. The banana trees paled by the cones of basalt. Yellow-eyed mynas flapped through the grove grass as the palm trees sighed and crossed one another, flinging themselves away in pieces. Then the rain roared inland, hot, big drops like spikes on my house, filling the rows of wide-open leaves.

The tide ran the flats in one slow motion. The tiers of lianas clustered deeper. She came from the edge of the hard-falling dawn, pretty, unseen, with the rain on her face. 'G'dai. Going over?' I thought, How do I know you?

From the jetty we followed a soft clay track that dropped through the bush to a clearing of bean fields and a pig in a stick-pen, snorting short questions. I heard a whoop and shouts ahead as we came to a palm-frond house on stilts.

'Oha, you lazy bunch! Got a chair for the big *papa-á*?'

'We do!' some voices called in English, with the rain flying off the porch in sheets.

'He's the one from the other side.' Moana explained me.

'Oh, yes, the man from the grove.' A tall woman smiled as she sat on the step. 'The house by the bad rocks. We know it.'

'How long you been here, man?' A sightless granny tapped me and squinted.

'Half a year,' I said. It vanished.

'Tom Wilkov thinks he's a funny bugger.' Moana laughed and folded her arms. Their open faces leaned forward, touching. The hidden children came out and stared at the rings of joining water.

We went to the landing while the sea was high, a day like the others with church bells and singing.

I painted the lizards on the sun-spotted branches and the blots of hibiscus hanging beside me. The tin roof creaked in the clouds' great shadows. Mangoes knocked on the limestone wall.

I drew the little frangipani trees, pink and white blossoms low in the boulders. I pulled back the mats of taro to see them, and the seagulls giggled and shrieked from the gate.

I met her on the beach and the islets of reeds, silent in the tossing, invisible days, alone on the tattered leaves in the sun.

Father John came to my house one Friday, a definite sight on the coral walk, with a breadfruit on his scythe and his black cassock striding. He stopped for a moment to ask how I was, waiting half-turned, with his white hair and waist cord still blowing away.

'Getting on all right, are you? And how is the artwork?'

Father John always asked the same questions, and they all had to do with me getting on. Sometime soon I would finish my paintings, get right on around them – and my hammock and the veranda boards I was nailing – and then, you see, I'd leave the island.

I shrugged and answered some flippant thing. Cramped, dour man – how was he here outside my house, bent like a threat in the still, red evening?

Then Tom Wilkov closed up his debt book. 'Can't help you, mate. You're in eighty dollars.' How did he get such a price in that place?

Not right away, but after some days, the policeman rode up through the grove on his pony. He would have a look at my visa today. He'd come in the heat and wanted to see it. Who had stirred him to be there and hold out his hand, asking for papers nobody had?

The *Tonga Roa* came on a Monday, bound for Tahiti with no other stops. The bells at the mission rang all morning and everyone gathered down on the sand, riding and walking in bright, slow groups.

The launch was ready with my suitcase and easel, and a chain of piled rowboats was tied to the pier. Moana leaned on a post by the store, happy where she was in the noise of the boat day. Then she went with her friends to the picked-over church-yard, sat in the flame tree, just as it pleased her.

BIOGRAPHICAL NOTES

SCOULAR ANDERSON was born in 1946 and brought up in Argyll. He studied at the Glasgow School of Art, then worked in London for seven years as an illustrator. He now lives in Glasgow, teaching art, illustrating books, painting and writing.

WILLIAM ANDREW was born in Glasgow in 1931. He taught English in London and Glasgow, and in the 1970s had several radio plays and two stage plays produced. In 1979, with the help of a Scottish Arts Council bursary, he began writing full-time. Since then he has worked mainly for television – three half-hour plays in STV's *Preview* series, various school programmes and many episodes of the serial *Take the High Road*.

MOIRA BURGESS was born in Campbeltown in 1936 and is a full-time writer and mother. Her novel *The Day Before Tomorrow* was published in 1971. She compiled *The Glasgow Novel: a bibliography* (1972: second edition forthcoming) and has just co-edited *Streets of Stone*, an anthology of Glasgow short stories. For some years she wrote mainly articles, but a Scottish Arts Council bursary in 1982 encouraged her to return to fiction, which she finds much more enjoyable.

FELICITY CARVER (Felicity Ivory) was born in Edinburgh in 1945 and has lived mostly in Scotland. A number of her short stories have been published by, among others, the *New Edinburgh Review* and *Punch*. She is married with two children.

IAIN CRICHTON SMITH was born on the island of Lewes in 1928. He is a full-time writer, working in both Gaelic and English, and has published novels, collections of short stories, poems and plays in both languages. His most recent collection of poetry is called *The Exiles*, and was the Poetry Book Society choice for summer 1984. He is married.

ELSPETH DAVIE was born in Ayrshire and went to school in Edinburgh, studied at university and art college and taught painting for several years. She lived for a while in Ireland before returning to Scotland. She has published three novels: *Providings, Creating a Scene, Climbers on a Stair*, and four collec-

171

tions of short stories: *The Spark, The High Tide Talker, The Night of the Funny Hats* and *A Traveller's Room*. She received Arts Council Awards in 1971 and 1977 and the Katherine Mansfield Short Story Prize in 1978. She is married and has one daughter.

RICHARD DINGWALL was born in Dundee in 1951. He has lived in New Zealand since 1980, and has hitherto only published work in that country.

DOUGLAS DUNN comes from Inchinnan and lives in Tayport. He has published six books of verse, the most recent being *Elegies* (Faber & Faber, 1985). His first collection of stories is *Secret Villages* (Faber & Faber, 1985).

RONALD FRAME was born in Glasgow in 1953, and educated there and at Oxford. His first novel, *Winter Journey*, was published by the Bodley Head in 1984; it was joint winner of the first Betty Trask Award. A collection of his short stories, *Watching Mrs Gordon*, was published by the Bodley Head in 1985; 'Paris' also appears in this collection, and has been dramatized for BBC 2.

ENID GAULDIE is married to an architect, has three children, works as a temporary, part-time lecturer at Duncan of Jordanstone College of Art, Dundee, and has been writing all her life. She is currently working on a collection of short stories.

ALAN D. KERR was born in 1948 and educated at Allan Glen's School, Glasgow. He lives in Milngavie, and embarked on creative writing in 1981. He is unmarried, and works in the hotel industry.

MORAG MACINNES was born in 1950 in Stromness in the Orkney Isles. She graduated from Edinburgh University to become a part-time further education teacher. She writes when she can.

BRIAN MCCABE was born in 1951 in Edinburgh, where he now lives. He has published three collections of poetry, most recently *Spring's Witch* (The Mariscat Press), and his poems and short stories have appeared in various periodicals and anthologies. He was awarded a writer's bursary by the Scottish Arts Council in 1980. He is presently writer-in-residence for Stirling District Libraries.

WILLIAM MILLER was born in Glasgow in 1928, and now lives in Edinburgh where he works as an engineer, employed by the same company for the past twenty-six years. Two of his short stories have been broadcast by the BBC but this is his first time in print. He has a wife, three children and one grandson.

BIOGRAPHICAL NOTES

CHRIS RETZLER was born and brought up in England and has lived in Germany and the USA. In 1982 he moved to Scotland from America with a Liberal Arts degree from Evergreen University. He now lives and works in Edinburgh and writes fiction in his spare time.

BRENDA SHAW is a New Englander who has lived and worked in Scotland for over twenty years. During her career in medical sciences she has published a textbook and over thirty research papers under her married name. Her poems have appeared in a number of British magazines. She is co-editor of the poetry broadsheet *Blind Serpent*, and editor of *Seagate II*, an anthology of poetry by writers with a Dundee connection, published by Taxus Press, Durham, in October 1984. She is married to a university lecturer and has two children.

JACKSON WEBB was born in Colorado and has lived in Galloway for the past twelve years. His stories have appeared on Radio 3 and in Scottish Arts Council collections, *Words, Blackwood's, New Writing Scotland* 1983 and 1984, and the *Scottish Review*. His first book, *The Last Lemon Grove* (Weidenfeld) was chosen by George Mackay Brown as *Scotsman*'s Book of the Year. He received the Tom-Gallon Award, a Scottish Arts Council Bursary, in 1981, has been tutor for the Galloway and Skye Writers' Workship, and was Writer-in-Residence for Yorkshire Arts in 1983–4. He has spent two years living in New Zealand and the Cook Islands.